DANIEL H. WILSON

GUARDIAN ANGELS & OTHER MONSTERS

Daniel H. Wilson is the bestselling author of *The Clockwork Dynasty, Robopocalypse, Robogenesis,* and *Amped,* among others. A Cherokee citizen, he was born in Tulsa, Oklahoma, and earned a B.S. in computer science from the University of Tulsa and a Ph.D. in robotics from Carnegie Mellon University in Pittsburgh. He lives in Portland, Oregon.

GUARDIAN ANGELS & OTHER MONSTERS

GUARDIAN ANGELS

& OTHER

MONSTERS

STORIES

DANIEL H. WILSON

VINTAGE BOOKS

A Division of Penguin Random House LLC

New York

A VINTAGE BOOKS ORIGINAL, MARCH 2018

Grateful acknowledgment is made to Association for
Computing Machinery, Inc. for permission to reprint
"Future Tense: Garden of Life" by Daniel H. Wilson,
originally published in *Communications of the ACM*
(Vol. 57, No. 10) on September 23, 2014. Reprinted by
permission of Association for Computing Machinery, Inc.

Several stories first appeared in the following publications: "The Blue
Afternoon That Lasted Forever" in *Carbide Tipped Pens* (Tor Books), "The
Executor" in *The Mad Scientist's Guide to World Domination* (Tor Books),
"Helmet" in *Armored* (Baen Books), "Foul Weather" in *Nightmare Magazine*
(December 2012, Issue 3), "The Nostalgist" as a Kindle Single on Tor.com,
"Parasite: A Robopocalypse Story" in *21st Century Dead* (St. Martin's Press),
and "God Mode" in *Press Start to Play* (Vintage Books).

Library of Congress Cataloging-in-Publication Data
Names: Wilson, Daniel H. (Daniel Howard), 1978– author.
Title: Guardian angels & other monsters : stories / by Daniel H. Wilson.
Description: New York : Vintage Books, 2017.
Identifiers: LCCN 2017028673 | ISBN 9781101972014 (pbk.)
Classification: LCC PS3623.I57796 A6 2017 | DDC 813/.6—dc23
LC record available at https://lccn.loc.gov/2017028673

**Vintage Books Trade Paperback ISBN: 978-1-101-97201-4
eBook ISBN: 978-1-101-97202-1**

Book design by Elizabeth A. D. Eno

www.vintagebooks.com

Printed in the United States of America
10 9 8 7 6 5 4 3 2 1

For Judy & Mark
Thanks for Maniac Mansion.

Character is destiny.

—Heraclitus

CONTENTS

GUARDIAN ANGELS & OTHER MONSTERS

MISS GLORIA

He taught me to go with him through pathless
deserts, dragging me on with mighty stride, and
to laugh at sight of the wild beasts, nor tremble
at the shattering of rocks by rushing torrents
or at the silence of the lonely forest.

—*The Achilleid* (94 CE)

The fairy house sprouts from a moss-covered tree trunk,
small but perfectly formed, sheltered by the spotted cupola
of a fey toadstool.

Nestled in dewy curls of turf, the miniature house has
been carefully pieced together from a stockpile of twigs orga-
nized by diameter and broken to the same length. Tiny flat
stones form a path leading to its door.

On his knees in the dirt, Chiron, named for the mythi-
cal Greek centaur, tutor to Achilles, leans over the mossy
landscape.

The robot moves gracefully, limbs and torso plated in

contoured pads over an economy of smooth silver strut-work. Sculpted into lines of classic musculature, each pale plate is comfortable to touch, devoid of pinch points, and easy to clean. Chiron is often smeared with spaghetti sauce or flecked with waxy streaks of crayon by the end of the day, though his infinite patience and love never waver.

The girl beside him, her knees dirty under a maroon sundress, is called Miss Gloria. She is six years old, weighs thirty-nine pounds, and is forty-six inches tall. As a specimen of little girl, she is largely unremarkable. Instead, the incredible aspects of her life come from the intersection of power and politics that finds its locus in her family. As a powerful man surrounded by enemies, Gloria's father entrusts his daughter only to an ally he has built himself.

To that end, he has spared no expense.

Chiron's most amazing attributes are not manifest in his elegantly sculpted form, but in the curious patterns of the mind. His thinking and memory are infinitely adaptable, self-preserving, and capable of extracting meaning and wisdom from whichever hardware happens to be available.

Of primary concern to Chiron is, of course, Miss Gloria's physical safety. After that comes her emotional development, confidence, and self-esteem. He intends to ensure that Miss Gloria someday realize her full potential as a grown woman.

Chiron is well aware that he will be discarded long before reaching this goal, and he is content. He knows that before a sculpture is completed, the scaffolding must fall away.

Crouched at his side, shoulder to shoulder, Miss Gloria knows only that Chiron is an excellent playmate. Not a friend—not exactly—but a presence whose measured voice is steady and constant, if a bit stern. Gloria loves her mentor purely—he is as much a fixture in her life as the rising of the sun and the sight of the constellations each night. In his own way, the machine also loves the girl. Miss Gloria is his life's work, and she is coming along wonderfully.

A bright red holly berry tumbles from the little girl's cupped hands.

"Look, Ky," she says with conspiratorial flair. "Poison berries."

Slipping, she drops the rest of the berries. They plummet like cannonballs, knocking twigs from the hut's roof.

"Careful, Miss Gloria," advises Chiron. "The fairy kings and queens won't appreciate a broken castle."

"Then fix it," demands Gloria.

"Is that a kind way to ask?" asks Chiron.

"*Now*," says Gloria, and she plants a small fist against Chiron's padded thigh.

"I think you should try on your own," Chiron says, crossing his arms and standing up. "And then I will help."

"But I can't do it," she says, eyeing the slender twigs. Gloria wraps an arm around Chiron's calf. "They're too small."

The machine does not budge.

With a sigh, Gloria crouches closer to the fairy house. Tongue peeking from the corner of her mouth, she succeeds in picking up a twig. Dropping it, she knocks down the rest of the hut, twigs tumbling from their perches.

"I *told* you, Ky," she says, sitting up. "*Now* will you fix it?"

Chiron does not respond.

"Do it for me," she insists. "It's your *job*."

"I am your teacher, Miss Gloria," says Chiron, closing his eyes and turning away theatrically. "My job is to let go."

Gloria rolls her eyes and punches the leg again, a little grin squirming into the corners of her mouth.

"Fix it," she begs. "I'll give you candy."

"Someday you will be alone and will have to rely upon yourself," says Chiron.

"Please, Chiron," begs Gloria. She pronounces his name in exaggerated syllables, *Ky-ron*. "Pretty please?"

Chiron opens one eye, looking down his long nose at the little girl. He is scanning her face for any trace of deceit. Her growing smile remains contained for the moment, though it threatens to escape.

Satisfied, Chiron leans over and reaches for her.

A man in black walks around the corner of the yard, a long weapon held high, stock tucked into his armored shoulder. Staring down the length of the kinetic battle rifle, the man's face is wrapped in a flat tactical mask studded with pinhole cameras and striped with mesh. Chiron pauses, still leaning over the little girl, arms extended to swoop her up.

The man pulls his trigger.

Three electromagnetically accelerated slugs hiss from

the barrel and flicker across the yard. Lancing into Chiron's chest, the armor-piercing rounds make a sound like pennies hitting a glass countertop, spraying wreckage as they eviscerate the dumbstruck robot.

The little girl is still smiling up at her best friend, reaching for his neck and not understanding why his features are frozen in place.

Staggered, the machine sags to his knees. Arms slack, his hands lie palm up on the ground. Chiron blinks once, head weaving as he loses power.

"Run away now, Miss Gloria," he says. *"Please."*

But Gloria doesn't obey. Hurt on her face, she watches Chiron topple over and collapse across the remains of the fairy house.

"Ky?" she asks. "Chiron?"

The gentle expression of concern never leaves the machine's face, even as his body slumps to the ground. Thin wisps of smoke curl from the scattered holes in his chest carapace.

Chiron dies at Miss Gloria's feet, there in the little backyard.

The girl shakes the fallen machine, panic in her voice, urging Chiron to wake up as a trotting shadow grows behind her.

A black-sleeved arm wraps around her chest and lifts her away.

Through a gauze of long hair and fear, Gloria does not see the bodies of her perimeter security detail, the men and women who are sprawled where they fell, their complicated armor melted to their bodies in glistening stripes of heat.

The laser strike took place from a distant hill. The necessary equipment was expensive, but effective.

The mercenary designated "Alpha" is relieved the mentor robot succumbed so quickly to a straight kinetic loadout. An unknown model with unknown security capabilities, the machine called "Chiron" represented a potential quandary.

You never know what these military contractors put into their machines.

Surveying the scene through the tactical battle visor over his face, Alpha scans for body heat or vibration or electromagnetic interference. He pauses at the sight of a flickering pulse guttering in the shell of the robot, but dismisses it. His subordinates Bravo and Charlie are arriving in a black SUV, their identities cloaked by thermally shielded balaclavas.

Alpha shoves the squirming child into the back of the vehicle. Charlie takes the girl in his sinewy mechanical arms—robotic replacements after some mission gone terribly wrong. Meanwhile, Bravo clambers into the passenger seat to make room for Alpha.

In the back, Gloria is shouting the name of the dead machine. She is kicking, fighting to reach the window. As a hand goes over her mouth, she glimpses her friend's body, eyes open, still lying on its side in the yard.

The vehicle speeds away, tires spraying clumps of manicured turf.

In the damp grass, an equation is unfolding. An algorithm wends its way through Chiron's failing mind, collecting his vital processes. The experience, memories, and personality of the machine gather in a cocoon of mathematics. And consuming the robot's last spark of electricity, the code tenses itself to leap. . . .

*** *Reboot.* ***

Chiron opens his eyes.

Something is wrong. Very wrong.

The pain of dying is great, but this world has not let go so easily. Though he has suffered a mortal wound, Chiron lives. The ground seems far away now, the entire city sprawling in a blur under a taut horizon.

In front of him, a column of red strutwork spears away into blue sky.

Diagnostics are offline. The usual stream of data is missing from Chiron's peripheral vision. Instead, he sees a simplistic array of wind speed and temperature and force vectors applied to various parts of a body he does not recognize. Within the data, Chiron resolutely picks out the contours of his now gargantuan physique.

A construction crane.

Chiron tries to blink and nothing happens. A seagull lands on his strut, pecking at its wing and leaning into a sporadic breeze. The quivering red arm supports a pallet of dense concrete tubing by a steel cable. Chiron lowers his gaze to see the city spread out in miniature, like one of Miss Gloria's wooden train sets.

Miss Gloria.

The strut begins to swing—slow at first, but gaining speed. Disturbed, the seagull flaps against a growing wind, feathers ruffled. The city scrolls past. Far below, Chiron spots a familiar backyard. And though his silver body is lying dead there, the coiled equation of Chiron's intellect has hurled itself into the void.

Below, a black vehicle speeds down the block.

Miss Gloria, thinks Chiron. *Her physical safety is compromised. There is no time to consider what has happened.*

Focusing his thoughts, Chiron-crane wills his arm to slow its turn. The pendulous load swings wildly. Far below, a smattering of brightly colored construction workers streak away like beads of Miss Gloria's milk used to spill off Chiron's soft plastic arm.

Not my arm. Not anymore.

Trundling forward like a beetle, the SUV slows and stops at a red light under the shadow of the crane. Ten meters above the street, delivery drones flicker along their routes in stuttering lines. The stoplight changes and the SUV creeps forward.

Chiron-crane makes a decision.

Now.

The seagull leaps into flight.

Springing back, the crane arm releases its heavy load. A pallet of concrete tubes sails through the air. It collapses across the intersection with a mushrooming explosion of gray dust and debris. Seconds later, the jarring smack of impact echoes up.

Delivery drones scatter like bathtub toys under Miss Gloria's pudgy fist.

The weight differential was too much. Vector readouts appear and spin crazily in Chiron-crane's peripheral vision. The horizon is leaping up and down as the camera shudders. Struts are popping. Metal is screaming.

The cars below are stuck in a sudden snarl of traffic and panicked pedestrians, some of them watching the spectacle and others running, diving for cover in the shadow of the bucking crane.

Chiron-crane watches without emotion as the sky fills his vision. The moan of wind grows over the tortured squeal of metal.

I am falling, thinks Chiron. *Too fast.*

The world vibrates as the back of Chiron-crane's head plows into another building. His colossal body shudders as it slouches against the side of the half-built skyscraper. Abruptly, his sight goes black.

And for the second time today, Chiron dies.

*** *Reboot.* ***

Reeling, Chiron tries to find himself.

In the darkness, he hears a small sound that causes great

consternation. It is the sound of a little girl sniffling, trying to contain sobs. Chiron recalls that Miss Gloria has a habit of pressing her hands over her mouth when she is crying but does not want to be crying, as if she could push the emotions back inside.

The world appears, upside down, flattened and smeared into a dish. Above a black plain, elongated shapes of traffic flicker past in candle wax streaks. Emergency lights flicker, and Chiron recognizes the receding image of a fallen crane as it is left behind. This is the eye of an omnidirectional camera—a conical mirror showing a 360-degree view around the black SUV. The vehicle is moving fast, speeding through city traffic.

Like some kind of exotic insect, Chiron-car opens a multitude of eyes and observes the street, curbs, and, finally, the interior of the vehicle.

Miss Gloria.

She is crying but unhurt, sitting beside an armored mercenary in the backseat while two more soldiers sit in the front. The driver is still wearing an armored tactical visor. His hands are tight on the steering wheel.

This is the one who killed me, thinks Chiron.

"What the fuck *was* that?" asks the passenger. "How could that happen? Cranes don't just fall—"

"It's a coincidence," says the driver. "Doesn't change our plan."

Stretching his muscles and his mind, Chiron-car feels the velocity of his tires and their heat against the pavement.

Concentrating, he cuts the acceleration.

"Why are we stopping?" asks the passenger.

In the back, Gloria cries out. An artificial hand goes back over her mouth.

"Not going to tell you again."

Her tears cascade over the plastic ridges of the man's fingers.

Fighting the grip of the human driver, the SUV's steering wheel pulls, guiding the vehicle to the side of the road. Engine still purring, it stops. The hazard lights turn on, and the onboard emergency call light illuminates.

"Hit the gas," urges the passenger. "Get us out of here!"

"I'm trying," says the driver. "It's gone to autopilot."

Every light on the dashboard illuminates at once, the radio babbling through stations until it settles on static.

"We're hacked. We've gotta be hacked—"

Thunk, thunk, thunk.

Chiron-car locks his doors, one after another.

The driver yanks his door handle but nothing happens. He jams a thumb into the window control and again nothing happens. The men are trapped inside, with emergency services on the way.

The voice of a dead machine rises over the speakers, even and calm.

"Miss Gloria," it says. "I am here."

The little girl's eyes open wide. Shrugging her head away from the palm over her mouth, she squeals.

"Chiron!"

"Help is on the way," says the voice.

"Shit shit shit," moans the passenger.

The driver remains calm, methodically running his fingers over the dashboard. Abruptly, he drops a gloved fist into a pinhole camera, shaking the image and blinding one of Chiron-car's many eyes.

"It's the nanny robot," says the man in back with artificial arms. "Must be a caster."

"We've got to get away from anything with processing power," says the driver.

Chiron opens another set of eyes. He looks down from the ceiling, through a cheap occupancy sensor. Not a clear image, just shapeless blobs moving about the cramped SUV.

"Where's the ECU?! The computer?" asks the driver.

His passenger stutters the words: "Passenger-side floorboard—"

The air inside the car shudders as the driver fires a kinetic pistol into the seat beside him. His passenger is shouting over the whining electromagnetic gunshots, voice shrill and in pain. The bullets are ricocheting up from the floorboard. Some of the bullets have gone into the man's thighs.

Chiron-car can feel the vibration through his metal spine.

"You shot me," the passenger is shouting. "You fucking shot me—"

Another bullet flickers through the man's temple and continues out the window. Chiron-car feels the warm heaviness of his circuits slowing, electricity surging as his consciousness shrinks down to a nothingness.

A door is being tugged open.

"C'mon, we're compromised—"

Abruptly, the camera view strobes white and black several times. Then the world blinks to black. There is nothing more here.

*** *Reboot* ***

A broad expanse of human skin stretches out in a freckled landscape, light teasing its edges like incipient dawn. Cobalt-blue eyes flicker back and forth, absorbing the information projected from the mask into pinprick black retinal wells.

Cheeks twitching, breathing hard, the man in black is running.

Having awoken inside the armored tactical helmet, Chironvisor takes a moment to bear witness to his adversary via inward-pointing cameras.

The mercenary has rough, reddish skin and stubbled hair that recedes from a sunburned forehead worn smooth as an old tire tread. The eyes are small and flinty and calculating, sunken above high, broad cheekbones and separated by a fleshy nose that bends to one side. An unruly brown-red moustache conceals his upper lip, then joins a red beard that spreads like a rash over his cheeks and the hard line of his mouth.

"Please, sir," says Chiron-visor. "You can still leave the girl and go peacefully."

A shuddering tremor passes through the facial landscape. A mountainous frown erupting from the brow ridge. Skin folding in pinched ravines.

"Not again," says the man, squeezing his eyes shut.

Groaning, he wrenches the blunt-faced helmet from his face. He throws the piece of high technology to the pavement and stomps on it. As the plastic and Kevlar and circuitry disintegrate, the tear-stained face of a little girl streaks by the camera.

A giant's boot heel arcs through the sky.

Miss Gloria—

*** *Reboot* ***

Waking up once again, Chiron tries to stand and falls. An engine buzzes, coiled deep in his breast, its power and vibration screaming through his arms and legs.

The world outside is upside down, blurred and spinning.

Chiron's sense of touch has expanded. Invisible lines of light spray from him into the environment, like fingers dragging lightly over a person's face. Orienting to the violet stripes of a laser range finder, Chiron levels his flight pattern. A line of other drones zip past, avoiding him with near-instinctive grace. A sidewalk meanders below, millimeter-sized canyons running through it.

Step on a crack, break your mother's back!

Miss Gloria used to shout those words, hopping between cracks on her string-bean legs. Wearing a paper crown on his head, Chiron would dutifully hop along behind her. With no mother, Chiron could foresee no harm in stepping on a crack. Gloria was also lacking in this respect, though Chiron chose not to mention the fact.

"Do you have a mommy and daddy, Chiron?" she asked once.

"No, Miss Gloria, I do not have parents."

"Who taught you?"

"I have had many, many teachers."

"Where are they?"

"They have gone. But I carry their lessons inside me."

Miss Gloria is near.

Leaning, Chiron-drone breaks rank and veers away from the sidewalk. The weight of a small package attached to his stomach throws off his motion, and he wobbles back and forth, zipping under a billboard and spinning through a crowd of startled pedestrians. Recovering, he surges higher into the air, stabilizing, sending out his light to find the precious girl somewhere below.

The black SUV is nearby, doors open. The passenger has fallen halfway out, facedown, on the road shoulder. His head is framed by a halo of shattered blue safety glass and a dark reddish puddle. Chiron-drone hurtles toward the broken vehicle, clenching his stomach talons to secure the package.

In the infrared spectrum, the cool imprints of boots emerge.

Speeding low over the pavement, Chiron-drone sees another body. The soldier from the backseat is lying spread-eagle in the scrubby grass. His mechanical arms have been shot to pieces—a precautionary measure. A worm trail of tire marks wends away from the dead bodies.

Somewhere nearby, a motorcycle engine screams.

Chiron-drone lifts, rotors twisting as he plunges ahead. A silver motorcycle accelerates away and Chiron-drone releases his package, the momentum pushing him forward into the contrail of the bike. Rotors thrumming, Chiron-drone edges closer.

Miss Gloria's familiar blond hair is whipping in the wind. She sits facing backward, her small arms wrapped around the man in black, hanging on for her life.

Hold on, Miss Gloria. I am coming.

Chiron-drone extends his small talons, scrabbling at the rear of the motorcycle seat. Latching on, he digs his talons into the leather. Pulling himself in tight, he hunkers down to let the wind flow past. The man in black does not notice the stowaway, busy guiding the motorcycle along a winding two-lane highway.

A green sign appears on the side of the road and Chiron-drone understands.

The mercenary is headed to the coast—away from all technology.

The wind and wailing of the engine combine to make a soothing song of static. A long time passes this way. Chiron-drone notices immediately when the engine drops an octave and the tires bite into rough gravel.

Trees lean over the misty road, their limbs covered in moss and hanging with cobwebs. The motorcycle turns onto a side road that leads to an empty overlook. The sun sinks through clawing branches, and the smell of saltwater grows strong.

The bike slows and stops near a metal railing. The broad gray back of the ocean rises from a cliff just beyond. Waves wash seaweed over a rocky beach below.

Chiron-drone drops off the back of the motorcycle.

Talons quietly scuttling on the ground, he rights himself. One by one, he runs each rotor and checks it for damage. With no technology nearby, there will likely be no more chances to save the girl.

The mercenary steps off the motorcycle. He sets the dazed little girl on the stripe of concrete beside the railing. Shaking his arms and stretching his legs, he pulls a phone from his pocket. He puts it to his head.

"Yeah. We're at the extraction point. Camp tonight, let daddy start to feel the pain. We make contact tomorrow morning."

Behind the mercenary, Chiron-drone lifts off, motors purring. Small talons hang from his belly. They are flexing one at a time, in preparation.

The mercenary stands at the railing, looking over the edge of the rocky cliff. The paint has peeled off the rusting metal, and the man decides to put his hands in his pockets. Beyond him, endless wrinkles of the sea glimmer under setting sunlight.

"Don't even think about running away, kid. You'll freeze to death out there."

"I want to go home," says Miss Gloria.

She has no more tears, her cheeks puffy and eyes blank with shock. Bruised shoulders peek from her sundress. The girl does not shiver in the damp evening.

"Yeah? We all want to go home—"

Chiron-drone streaks out, colliding with the man's face as he turns. Small talons clamp onto his cheeks. Rotors spin to maximum torque as gloved fingers close around his shining carapace. The plastic blades shatter on impact, slicing into the mercenary's forehead.

"Miss Gloria," announces the drone over a reedy speaker. "I am here."

Roaring, the man in black catches hold of the drone and pulls its scrabbling talons from his face. Parallel rows of blood well over his cheeks and forehead, eyes wide and wild and disbelieving as he looks down at the shivering hunk of plastic.

"Goddamn it!" he shouts, face tilting crazily as he throws the drone to the ground. Military boots fall over the helpless machine. Chiron-drone feels its casing splinter, his shattered rotors self-amputating, spraying plastic shards over the ground.

"Miss Gloria—"

"Die, you fucking piece of shit," comes the shout from above. The man runs a forearm over his face, looks at it, and sees his armored sleeve glistening with blood. Down comes the boot again.

"Fuck!"

*** *Reboot* ***

A vast black void opens up—an endless vista of failure and unmet expectations. Chiron is wondering whether this is true death when, once again, life blossoms in his heart.

Struggling to open his eyes, Chiron tries to move and cannot.

Rust-locked limbs are pinned to his sides. A weak battery flickers behind his eyelids like a failing pulse. Through a barely functioning ultrasonic array, Chiron feels the bones of heavy construction equipment around him.

Finally, a camera comes online.

Neck grating, Chiron looks down at his hands and sees a shovel. He is standing beside the empty two-lane highway, faint sunlight cutting through the mossy forest beyond. His power is low. Solar panels mounted on a nearby bulldozer have gotten dusty, and this machine hasn't been called into work over the winter.

Moving slowly, Chiron-worker coaxes his rusty bulk into taking a step.

Recognizing the driveway toward the campground, he pushes his legs through their motions, clutching the shovel against his chest. Slowly, loudly, he makes his way down the driveway until he sees the silhouette of a motorcycle parked next to a metal railing. A small campfire flickers in the dusk.

The mercenary stands up. His jacket is off now, and he has used his T-shirt to daub blood from his face. Miss Gloria cowers near the fire, arms wrapped around her knees. In the growing darkness, their faces are pale blurs.

"Wow!" shouts the man. "Wow. You just don't give up, huh?"

The man draws his kinetic pistol, standing with his legs wide. Behind him, the last gleam of sunlight settles dully over the ocean.

"We are officially in the middle of nowhere," says the man. His fingernails are rimed in dirt, sweat glistening under his eyes. "No place left for you to go. Nothing for you to do but die, *Chiron.*"

"Please," says Chiron-worker, advancing. The word comes in the low grate of a diagnostic voice.

The mercenary smiles at the clumsy gait of the rust-streaked robot. He knows military hardware, and this derelict machine is obviously not a threat. Nevertheless, Chiron-worker raises the shovel with shaking hands.

"I'm going to kill her, you know that?" asks the man. "After we get the ransom. You've truly fucked everything up. I hope you're happy about that."

Then he puts a bullet through Chiron-worker's forehead.

Built to clear brush and fill in potholes, this machine's processors are housed in its main body, leaving the head for sensing and human interaction purposes. Chiron is already leaning forward, running blindly.

Colliding with the man, Chiron-worker breaks the rotten shovel in half against his torso then wraps the mercenary in a bear hug. Struggling, he feels the bite of the metal fence at his thigh. He loses his grip on the man. Blind and deaf to the world, Chiron's gyroscope reports a constellation of angles and velocities.

He is falling through the sky.

Impact.

*** *End of Run.* ***

"Chiron!"

Gloria leans over the railing, lip quivering. Below, she sees the bad man. He is clinging to the rocky slope, bloody-faced, looking up at her with a snarl.

"Stay there, you little bitch!" he shouts, teeth bared.

Beyond him, the glittering remains of Chiron's body are spread over black rocks and frothy sand. Turning away, Gloria succumbs to tears. The grief comes so hard that her body is wracked with coughs, her curled fists scraping hard stone.

She thinks of Chiron's wise, kind face. Remembers his gentle voice.

And though she tries to ignore it, Gloria hears the grunting and cursing of the bad man. He is climbing the rocks. Soon, he will reach the top.

This time there will be no Chiron to save her.

Gloria lies on her side, chest convulsing with sobs. She is lost and hurt and alone. She is six years old.

Miss Gloria?

The voice is familiar.

"Ky," she whispers, wiping her nose on a forearm.

There is no response. Turning, Gloria sees the bad man's fingers close around the bottom rung of the metal railing. Both of his hands are clamped onto the rusting metal bar, knuckles white.

The metal curve of a broken shovel is nearby.

"Ky," she pleads. "Please."

Miss Gloria. I am here.

It *is* her teacher's voice, low and modulated, as calm as ever. Or maybe it's the whispering lap of unseen waves at the base of the cliff? Or the wind.

There is something you must do.

The girl turns her head, trying to deny what she knows is coming.

You must push the bad man's fingers away.

"No, no. It's not kind," she murmurs, or perhaps only thinks.

You must. Or he will hurt you.

Biting her lip, tears welling in her eyes, Gloria looks at the dirty fingers wrapped over the bottom rail. The man is hanging, cursing and struggling. He is gathering his strength to lunge higher.

Someday you will be alone.

She remembers Chiron's words and she can almost hear them in his voice.

. . . and will have to rely upon yourself.

The dirt-caked shovel rests on the pavement.

"This," she murmurs.

Good thinking, Miss Gloria.

She lifts the broken shovel in both hands, trembling. Raising it over her head, she closes her eyes and swings. Bringing it down as hard as she can, she feels the hard metal bounce from something soft and spongy.

Like fairy moss, imagines Gloria.

Someone, somewhere, is screaming hoarsely. Begging between shrieks. Gloria cannot hear the desperate cries over the sound of her own breathing and the rustle of her arms over her ears and, most important, over her teacher's calm voice.

You are doing such a good job, Miss Gloria. This is a very difficult thing, but you are a very strong girl.

Gloria smashes the shovel down again and again. She thinks maybe she hears a man crying for his mother and something warm and wet is spattering on her face but she keeps her eyes squeezed closed and only swings harder.

Finally, the shovel clangs against metal. Gloria stops and opens her eyes. The bad man's fingers have gone away from the railing.

She lays down the shovel.

"You did a good job, Gloria," she says to herself in a quiet, calm voice.

Distant waves crash on the rocks below, whispering to each other beyond the railing. Birds are calling in shrill voices across the lonely countryside. This place is cold and empty and growing dark, but the girl is not afraid.

Gloria is by herself, but she will never be alone again.

THE BLUE AFTERNOON THAT LASTED FOREVER

"It's late at night, my darling. And the stars are in the sky. That means it is time for me to give you a kiss. And an Eskimo kiss. And now I will lay you down and tuck you in, nice and tight, so you stay warm all night."

This is our mantra. I think of it like the computer code I use to control deep space simulations in the laboratory. You recite the incantation and the desired program executes.

I call this one "bedtime."

Marie holds her stuffed rabbit close, in a choke hold. In the dim light, a garden of blond hair grows over her pillow. She is three years old and smiling and she smells like baby soap. Her eyes are already closed.

"I love you, honey," I say.

As a physicist, it bothers me that I find this acute feeling of love hard to quantify. I am a man who routinely deals in singularities and asymptotes. It seems like I should have the mathematical vocabulary to express these things.

Reaching for her covers, I try to tuck Marie in. I stop when I feel her warm hands close on mine. Her brown eyes are black in the shadows.

"No," she says, "I do it."

I smile until it becomes a wince.

This version of the bedtime routine is buckling around the edges, disintegrating like a heat shield on reentry. I have grown to love tucking the covers up to my daughter's chin. Feeling her cool damp hair and the reassuring lump of her body, safe in her big-girl bed. Our routine in its current incarnation has lasted one year two months. Now it must change. Again.

I hate change.

"Okay," I murmur. "You're a big girl. You can do it."

Clumsily and with both hands, she yanks the covers toward her face. She looks determined. Proud to take over this task and exert her independence. Her behavior is consistent with normal child development according to the books I checked out from the library. Yet I cannot help but notice that this independence is a harbinger of constant unsettling, saddening change.

My baby is growing up.

In the last year, her body weight has increased 16 percent.

Her average sentence length has increased from seven to ten words. She has memorized the planets, the primary constellations, and the colors of the visible spectrum. Red orange yellow green blue indigo violet. These small achievements indicate that my daughter is advanced for her age, but she isn't out of the record books or into child genius territory. She's just a pretty smart kid, which doesn't surprise me. Intelligence is highly heritable.

"I saw a shooting star," she says.

"Really? What's it made of?" I ask.

"Rocks," she says.

"That's right. Make a wish, lucky girl," I reply, walking to the door.

I pause as long as I can. In the semidarkness, a stuffed bear is looking at me from a shelf. It is a papa teddy bear hugging its baby. His arms are stitched around the baby's shoulders. He will never have to let go.

"Sweet dreams," I say.

"Good night, Daddy," she says and I close the door.

The stars really are in Marie's bedroom.

Two years ago I purchased the most complex and accurate home planetarium system available. There were no American models. This one came from a Japanese company and it had to be shipped here to Austin, Texas, by special order. I also purchased an international power adapter plug, a Japanese-to-English translation book, and a guide to the major constellations.

I had a plan.

Soon after the planetarium arrived, I installed it in my bedroom. Translating the Japanese instruction booklet as best I could, I calibrated the dedicated shooting star laser, inserted the disc that held a pattern for the northern hemisphere, and updated the current time and season. When I was finished, I went into the living room and tapped my then-wife on the shoulder.

Our anniversary.

My goal was to create a scenario in which we could gaze at the stars together every night before we went to sleep. I am interested in astrophysics. She was interested in romantic gestures. It was my hypothesis that sleeping under the faux stars would satisfy both constraints.

Unfortunately, I failed to recall that I wear glasses and that my then-wife wore contact lenses. For the next week, we spent our evenings blinking up at a fuzzy Gaussian shotgun-spray of the Milky Way on our bedroom ceiling. Then she found the receipt for the purchase and became angry. I was ordered to return the planetarium and told that she would rather have had a new car.

That didn't seem romantic to me, but then again I'm not a domain expert.

My thin translation book did not grant me the verbal fluency necessary to negotiate a return of the product to Japan. In response, my then-wife told me to sell it on the Internet or whatever. I chose to invoke the "whatever" clause. I wrapped the planetarium carefully in its original packaging and put it into the trunk of my car. After that, I stored it in the equipment room of my laboratory at work.

Three months later, my then-wife informed me that she was leaving. She had found a job in Dallas and would try to visit Marie on the weekends but no promises. I immediately realized that this news would require massive life recalibrations. This was upsetting. I told her as such and my then-wife said that I had the emotional capacity of a robot. I decided that the observation was not a compliment. However, I did not question how me being a robot might affect my ability to parent a one-and-a-half-year-old. Contrary to her accusation, my cheeks were stinging with a sudden cold fear at the thought of losing my daughter. My then-wife must have seen the question in the surface tension of my face, because she answered it anyway.

She said that what I lacked in emotion, I made up for in structure. She said that I was a terrible husband, but a good father.

Then-wife kissed Marie on the head and left me standing in the driveway with my daughter in my arms. Marie did not cry when her mother left because she lacked the cognitive capacity to comprehend what had happened. If she had known, I think she would have been upset. Instead, my baby only grinned as her mother drove away. And because Marie was in such good spirits, I slid her into her car seat and drove us both to my laboratory. Against all regulations, I brought her into my work space. I dug through the equipment stores until I found the forbidden item.

That night, I gave my daughter the stars.

———

The cafeteria where I work plays the news during lunch. The television is muted but I watch it anyway. My plastic fork is halfway to my mouth when I see the eyewitness video accompanying the latest breaking news story. After that, I am not very aware of what is happening except that I am running.

I don't do that very much. Run.

In some professions, you can be called into action in an emergency. A vacationing doctor treats the victim of an accident. An off-duty pilot heads up to the cockpit to land the plane. I am not in one of those professions. I spend my days crafting supercomputer simulations so that we can understand astronomical phenomena that happened billions of years ago. That's why I am running alone. There are perhaps a dozen people in the world who could comprehend the images I have just seen on the television—my colleagues, fellow astrophysicists at research institutions scattered around the globe.

I hope they find their families in time.

The television caption said that an unexplained astronomical event has occurred. I know better than that. I am running hard because of it, my voice making a whimpering sound in the back of my throat. I scramble into my car and grip the hot steering wheel and press the accelerator to the floor. The rest of the city is still behaving normally as I weave through traffic. That won't last for long, but I'm thankful to have these few moments to slip away home.

My daughter will need me.

There is a nanny who watches Marie during the day. The nanny has brown hair and she is five feet four inches tall. She does not have a scientific mind-set but she is an artist in her spare time. When Marie was ten months old and had memorized all of her body parts (including the phalanges), I became excited about the possibilities. I gave the nanny a sheet of facts that I had compiled about the states of matter for Marie to memorize. I intentionally left off the quark-gluon plasma state and Bose-Einstein condensate and neutron-degenerate matter because I wanted to save the fun stuff for later. After three days I found the sheet of paper in the recycling bin.

I was a little upset.

Perez in the cubicle next to me said the nanny had done me a favor. He said Marie has plenty of time to learn about those things. She needs to dream and imagine and, I don't know, finger paint. It is probably sound advice. Then again, Perez's son is five years old and at the department picnic the boy could not tell me how many miles it is to the troposphere. And he says he wants to be an astronaut. Good luck, kid.

Oh, yes. Running.

My brain required four hundred milliseconds to process the visual information coming from the cafeteria television. Eighty milliseconds for my nervous system to respond to the command to move. It is a two-minute sprint to the parking lot. Then an eight-minute drive to reach home. Whatever happens will occur in the next thirty minutes and so there is no use in warning the others.

Here is what happened.

An hour and thirty-eight minutes ago, the sky blushed red as an anomaly streaked over the Gulf of Mexico. Bystanders described it as a smear of sky and clouds, a kind of glowing reddish blur. NASA reported that it perturbed the orbital paths of all man-made satellites, including the international space station. It triggered tsunamis along the equator and dragged a plume of atmosphere a thousand miles into the vacuum of space. The air dispersed in low pressure but trace amounts of water vapor froze into ice droplets. On the southern horizon, I can now see a fading river of diamonds stretching into space. I don't see the moon in the sky but that doesn't mean it isn't there. Necessarily.

All of this happened within the space of thirty seconds.

This is not an unexplained astronomical event. The anomaly had no dust trail, it was not radar detectable, and it caused a tsunami.

Oh, and it turned the sky red.

Light does funny things in extreme gravity situations. When a high-mass object approaches, every photon of light that reaches our eyes must claw its way out of a powerful gravity well. Light travels at a constant speed, so instead of slowing down, the photon sacrifices energy. Its wavelength drops down the visible spectrum: violet indigo blue green yellow orange red.

Redshifting.

I am running because only one thing could redshift our sky that much and leave us alive to wonder why our mobile

phones don't work. What passed by has to have been a pre-
viously theoretical class of black hole with a relatively small
planet-sized mass—compressed into a singularity poten-
tially as small as a pinprick. Some postulate that these entities are starving black holes that have crossed intergalactic
space and shrunk over the billions of years with nothing to
feed on. Another theory, possibly complementary, is that
they are random crumbs tossed away during the violence of
the big bang.

Perez in the next cubicle said I should call them "black
marbles," which is inaccurate on several fronts. In my papers,
I chose instead to call them pinprick-sized black holes.
Although Perez and I disagreed on the issue of nomencla-
ture, our research efforts brought consensus on one calcula-
tion: that the phenomenon would always travel in clusters.

Where there is one, more will follow.

Tornado sirens begin to wail as I careen through my sub-
urban neighborhood. The woman on the car radio just
frantically reported that something has happened to Mars.
The planet crust is shattered. Astronomers are describing
a large part of the planet's mass as simply missing. What's
left behind is a cloud of expanding dirt and rapidly cooling
magma, slowly drifting out of orbit and spreading into an
elliptical arc.

She doesn't say it out loud, but it's dawning on her: we
are next.

People are standing in their yards now, on the sidewalks and grass, eyes aimed upward. The sky is darkening. The wind outside the car window is whispering to itself as it gathers occasionally into a thin, reedy scream. A tidal pull of extreme gravity must be doing odd things to our weather patterns. If I had a pen and paper, I could probably work it out.

I slam on the brakes in my driveway to avoid hitting the nanny.

She is standing barefoot, holding a half-empty sippy cup of milk. Chin pointed at the sky. Stepping out of the car, I see my first pinprick-sized black hole. It is a reddish dot about half the intensity of the sun, wrapped in a halo of glowing, superheated air. It isn't visibly moving so I can't estimate its trajectory. On the southern horizon, the crystallized plume of atmosphere caused by the near miss still dissipates.

It really is beautiful.

"What is it?" asks the nanny.

"Physics," I say, going around the car and opening my trunk. "You should go home immediately."

I pull out a pair of old jumper cables and stride across the driveway. Marie is standing just inside the house, her face a pale flash behind the glass storm door. Inside, I lift my daughter off the floor. She wraps her legs around my hip and now I am running again, toys crunching under my feet, my daughter's long hair tickling my forearm. The nanny has put it into a braid. I never learned how to do that. Depending on the trajectory of the incoming mass, I may not ever have the chance.

"What did you do today?" I ask Marie.

"Played," she says.

Trying not to pant, I crack open a few windows in the house. Air pressure fluctuations are a certainty. I hope that we only have to worry about broken glass. There is no basement to hide in here, just a cookie-cutter house built on a flat slab of concrete. But the sewer main is embedded deep into the foundation. In the worst case, it will be the last thing to go.

I head to the bathroom.

"Wait here for just a second," I say, setting Marie down in the hallway. Stepping into the small bathroom, I wind up and violently kick the wall behind the toilet until the drywall collapses. Dropping to my knees, I claw out chunks of the drywall until I have exposed the main sewer line that runs behind the toilet. It is a solid steel pipe maybe six inches in diameter. With shaking hands, I shove the jumper cable around it. Then I wedge myself between the toilet and the outside wall and sit down on the cold tile floor, the jumper cables under my armpits anchoring me to the ground. This is the safest place I can find.

If the black hole falling toward us misses the planet, even by a few thousand miles, we may survive. If it's a direct hit, we'll share the fate of Mars. At the sonic horizon, sound won't be able to escape from it. At the event horizon, neither will light. Before that can happen we will reach a Lagrange point as the anomaly cancels out Earth's gravity. We will fall into the sky and be swallowed by that dark star.

The anomaly was never detected, so it must have come from intergalactic space. The Oort cloud is around a light-year out, mostly made of comets. The Kuiper asteroid belt is on the edge of the solar system. Neither region had enough density to make the black hole visible. I wonder what we were doing when it entered our solar system. Was I teaching Marie the names of dead planets?

"Daddy?" asks Marie.

She is standing in the bathroom doorway, eyes wide. Outside, a car engine revs as someone speeds past our house. A distant, untended door slams idiotically in the breeze. Marie's flowery dress shivers and flutters over her scratched knees in the restless calm.

"Come here, honey," I say in my most reassuring voice. "Come sit on my lap."

Hesitantly, she walks over to me. The half-open window above us is a glowing red rectangle. It whistles quietly as air is pulled through the house. I tie the greasy jumper cable cord in a painfully tight knot around my chest. I can't risk crushing her lungs, so I wrap my arms around Marie. Her arms fall naturally around my neck, hugging tight. Her breath is warm against my cheek.

"Hold on to your daddy very tight," I say. "Do you understand?"

"But why?" she asks.

"Because I don't want to lose you, baby," I say and

my sudden swallowed tears are salty in the back of my throat.

Whips are cracking in the distance now. I hear a scream. Screams.

A gust of wind shatters the bathroom window. I cradle Marie closer as the shards of glass are sucked out of the window frame. A last straggler rattles in place like a loose tooth. The whip cracks are emanating from loose objects that have accelerated upward past the speed of sound. The *crack-crackcrack* sound is thousands of sonic booms. They almost drown out the frightened cries of people who are falling into the sky. Millions must be dying this way. Billions.

"What is that?" asks Marie, voice wavering.

"It's nothing, honey. It's okay," I say, holding her to me. Her arms are rubber bands tight around my neck. The roof shingles are rustling gently, leaping into the sky like a flock of pigeons. I can't see them but it occurs to me that the direction they travel will be along the thing's incoming trajectory. I watch that rattling piece of glass that's been left behind in the window frame, my lips pressed together. It jitters and finally takes flight *straight up*.

A fatal trajectory. A through-and-through.

"What's happening?" Marie asks, through tears.

"It's the stars, honey," I say. "The stars are falling."

It's the most accurate explanation I can offer.

"Why?" she asks.

"Look at Daddy," I say. I feel a sudden lightness, a gentle tug pulling us upward. I lean against the cables to make sure they are still tight. "Please look at your daddy. It will be okay. Hold on tight."

Nails screech as a part of the roof frame curls away and disappears. Marie is biting her lips to keep her mouth closed and nodding as tears course over her cheeks. I have not consulted the child development books but I think she is very brave for three years old. Only three trips around the sun and now the sun is going to end. Sol will be teased apart in hundred-thousand-mile licks of flame.

"My darling," I say. "Can you tell me the name of the planet that we live on?"

"Earth."

"And what is the planet with a ring around it?"

"S-Saturn."

"What are the rings made of?"

"Mountains of ice."

Maybe a sense of wonder is also a heritable trait.

"Are the stars—"

Something big crashes outside. The wind is shrieking now in a new way. The upper atmosphere has formed into a vortex of supersonic air molecules.

"Daddy?" screams Marie. Her lips are bright and bitten, tear ducts polishing those familiar brown eyes with saline. A quivering frown is dimpling her chin and all I can think of is how small she is compared to all this.

"Honey, it's okay. I've got you. Are the stars very big or very small?"

"Very big," she says, crying outright now. I rock her as we speak, holding her to my chest. The cables are tightening and the sewer main is a hard knuckle against my spine. Marie's static-charged hair is lifting in the fitful wind.

"You're right again. They look small, but they're very big. The stars are so very, very big."

A subsonic groan rumbles through the frame of the house. Through the missing roof I can see that trees and telephone poles and cars are tumbling silently into the red eye overhead. Their sound isn't fast enough to escape. The air in here is chilling as it thins but I can feel heat radiating down from that hungry orb.

Minutes now. Maybe seconds.

"Daddy?" Marie asks.

Her lips and eyes are tinged blue as her light passes me. I'm trying to smile for her but my lips have gone spastic. Tears are leaking out of my eyes, crawling over my temples and dripping up into the sky. The broken walls of the house are dancing. A strange light is flowing in the quiet.

The world is made of change. People arrive and people leave. But my love for her is constant. It is a feeling that cannot be quantified because it is not a number. Love is a pattern in the chaos.

"It is very late, my darling," I say. "And the stars are in the sky."

They are so very big.

"And that means it's time for me to give you a kiss. And an Eskimo kiss."

She leans up for the kiss by habit. Her tiny nose mushing into mine.

"And now . . ."

I can't do this.

"And now I will lay you down . . ."

Swallow your fear. You are a good father. Have courage.

"And tuck you in, nice and tight, so you stay warm all night."

The house has gone away from us and I did not notice. The sun is a sapphire eye on the horizon. It lays gentle blue shadows over a scoured wasteland.

And a red star still falls.

"Good night, my darling."

I hold her tight as we rise together into the blackness. The view around us expands impossibly and the world outside speeds up in a trick of relativity. A chaotic mass of dust hurtles past and disappears. In our last moment together, we face a silent black curtain of space studded with infinite unwavering pinpricks of light.

We will always have the stars.

JACK, THE DETERMINED

You see, sir, life is a series of misunderstandings.

—Denis Diderot,
Jacques the Fatalist and His Master (1785)

Jack sat next to the whirring copy machine in a cramped room at the Institut National Polytechnique de Langres. His Professor stood in front of the machine. The Professor held a thick book facedown and winced each time the bright light flashed from his thick glasses. Leaning against the wall, Jack idly held one hand near the machine and felt the heat of it radiating against his outstretched fingers.

Why were these two in France? Sadly, that is not up to me to decide. That is possibly regrettable, because if this were not a true story then there could be many amazing and terrible reasons. Maybe they were spies, copying documents describing a secret weapon? Maybe they were on the verge of a great discovery, which would be stolen from them and then recovered moments before disaster? Maybe not. Instead, they were ordinary participants at a prestigious technical conference. The truth is that the Professor had arrived only to deliver a report on a most important scientific work with his Jack, a most loyal and obedient student.

With a creaking noise and a frantic beeping, the copy machine stopped. The Professor groaned.

"Don't be angry," said Jack. "If the machine is broken, then it must have been written up above that it would happen. In the stars."

"That is very profound, Jack, but my presentation will be terrible if I have no handouts."

"It will be as it was meant to be. Nothing less."

"Or more," said the Professor, before pausing. "Jack, *you* are my presentation. We have only an hour left anyway. Let us forget the paper and go to the café."

The student and teacher sat at a small round table outside the café. The winter sunlight was dazzling and without heat. Jack squinted through it. The Professor sipped a cappuccino, gripping the cup gently between thick fingers and dipping his gray mustache in froth.

"Jack, my boy, I'm all nerves. You must tell me a story," said the Professor.

Jack considered his mentor's request for a mere instant

before making a decision. "Very well. I will tell you about something that happened to me this morning. In fact, it was a very distressing event."

Elbows fluttering, the Professor noisily placed his cup on the unsteady table. "Distressing, you say?"

"Most," replied Jack. "This morning I awoke in the hallway outside of our hotel room, standing up and already wearing my day's clothing."

"You don't say!" exclaimed the Professor.

"I *did* say! I have no recollection of how I arrived there. It occurred to me that I must have already eaten, because I had no appetite—"

"Ah! That explains why you had no breakfast."

"True, but I haven't yet arrived at the most distressing part of my story—"

At that moment, a woman in a bright yellow dress approached from the sidewalk. She lowered her sunglasses and waved a hand, opening and closing red-nailed fingers.

"Professor!" she called.

The Professor grunted and turned from Jack. He patted his chest, searching for errant eyeglasses. The woman clambered past silver tables, straining her dress as she squeezed between occupied chairs, and sat herself down between Jack and the Professor.

The smell of her perfume swept into the Professor's nostrils. The old man's nose fell to wrinkles and he swallowed a throbbing sneeze, his corduroyed knees beating a staccato rhythm on the underside of the table.

"Sorry to interrupt," said the woman. "My name is Gretchen Hall. I'm in town for the conference. I've been following your work for years, Professor."

The Professor's chest expanded. "Well. Yes, I—"

"Oh my," said Gretchen. "Is this Jack?"

"Indeed," sniffed Jack.

The waitress approached the table and addressed Gretchen, holding out a lazily flapping menu. "Would you like to make a choice, madame?"

"Oh, no thank you," she said.

"And you, monsieur?" asked the waitress.

Jack looked at the Professor. "Yes, I suppose I would," he said.

"No. No, he cannot," said the Professor.

"Well!" huffed Jack. "I think that I *would,* and therefore I shall. I am quite capable of ordering a drink on my own, Professor."

"So this is the famous Jack," said Gretchen Hall. "You two make quite a pair!"

"Thank you, Gretchen," said Jack, extending his hand. A smile twitched on his lips. "You know, we haven't been properly introduced."

"I am ordering you *not* to order that coffee!" exclaimed the Professor, surprising himself with his own vehemence.

Jack scowled at his mentor. "My fate is written in the stars, Professor. A domain that slightly exceeds your grasp. Or do you flatter yourself to think that you can control my every action?"

Jack sniffed angrily and looked away.

The waitress put a hand on her hip and sighed. "Monsieur? What will you choose?"

"You are my student," said the Professor. "You will obey me because I am your professor and you are my Jack and what I tell you to do is what you will do."

"You *look* like my professor. You *sound* like my professor. But we both know who the teacher is. We can pretend to the contrary all you like, and that suits me perfectly. But you cannot place knowledge in my head like placing direction in a play or equations on paper. Just know that it is pretend—this control of yours—and that I can do whatever I wish whenever I wish and wherever I wish!"

Jack slammed his hands onto the table, rattling the Professor's cup and causing Gretchen to startle and drop her sunglasses.

"Waitress," Jack said. "Bring me an espresso. And you, Professor, you tell me, where will you be in one hour without *your* Jack?"

What a row! Now, reader, what should happen next? Perhaps the Professor will become enraged, kick over the flimsy table, and wrap his fingers around the throat of his impudent student? Or maybe he will simply stand and walk away, catch a flight back across the ocean, and abandon his star pupil? Alas, I believe that Jack's words held truth. As often happens to normal people at inopportune moments, the Professor sat speechless, filled with impotent indignation.

The waitress, on the other hand, thanked Jack and left

to fetch the drink, happy to have finally received a cogent order.

"Jack?" asked Gretchen. "I had no idea that you could drink?"

The Professor found his voice. He sputtered, "He can't!"

"I can!"

"You can't!"

"I can—"

The waitress returned. "I am so sorry," she said. "But the machine has broken."

Everyone at the table sat quietly. The waitress took the opportunity to step away.

"It must have been written up above," said Jack, quietly. "You were right, Professor. I apologize. I was not meant to drink coffee today."

The Professor sat up and brushed his whiskers with one hand. He glanced at Gretchen; she watched Jack intensely.

"Yes. Well. Do please finish telling me your story," said the Professor.

"Well, as I was saying," continued Jack, "I found myself standing in the hallway, fully clothed and with no recollection of how I got there. Facing the wall, I saw the most disturbing image painted only inches from my eyes. The figure was of a skull and crossbones, and it filled my entire field of view. Surely, this is a bad omen."

"An omen certainly," said the Professor. "Your feet choose strange places to take you."

"Stepping away from the wall, I realized that I was standing in front of a metal cabinet. In my left hand I was holding a black cord that went under the door and into the cabinet."

The Professor leaned forward, dipping his shirtsleeve in his coffee. "You *did not* open the cabinet!"

Reader, what could be in the cabinet? It has certainly upset the Professor. In truth, I cannot say. I simply do not know. But it must be a horrible thing indeed. Or perhaps utterly mundane?

"No," replied Jack. "I was confused. My mind was racing like a spooked horse. To be quite honest, I was so frightened that I dropped the cord and came straight away to meet you and make preparations for the speech."

Gretchen spoke. "It sounds like an electrical cabinet, to me. They're imprinted with the skull and bones as a warning. I wonder why this should surprise you—"

"What?" interrupted the Professor. "Of course it is a surprise! To wake fully clothed!"

"But—"

The Professor stood suddenly, again banging his knees into the table. "It is time to go, Jack," he announced, holding one hand up to block the sharp sunlight from his eyes. "The presentation will begin shortly. Good day to you, Gretchen."

And then the Professor abruptly walked away from the table. Jack shrugged to Gretchen, grinning, and dutifully followed his mentor.

———

Jack and the Professor stood together on the narrow wing of a stage, out of sight of the audience, ensconced in thick velvet curtains. Onstage, a white-haired man in a black suit stood behind a wooden podium. The stage was bare aside from the podium, a blackboard, and an odd table. The white-haired man waved his hands excitedly. He spoke eloquently and grandly of the Professor and his important scientific work. Jack blew air through his nose and traced his eyes with disinterest across the side of the man's head.

"Why should I even bother coming to this presentation?" asked Jack in a whisper. "Are you not even capable of describing the results that I have collected through countless hours of hard work?"

The Professor adjusted his bow tie. The faint reverberation of hundreds of colliding hands emanated from the audience. The Professor looked mutely at Jack, then turned and stepped onto the stage, wincing under the bright lights. He picked up a piece of chalk and wrote on the blackboard: *"Jacques: Un Homme Mécanique avec un Cerveau Artificiel."*

A slow, deep wave of applause rolled in from the audience and died away.

The Professor turned to Jack, beckoned him to emerge. Jack walked out onto the stage slowly, nonchalant. The student ignored the myriad sparkling eyes hidden in the glare of the spotlights. He approached the Professor and looked past him to the blackboard. He read the words.

Jack looked at the Professor with wide, confused eyes.

"Mécanique? What?" he whispered.

"Jack, please sit," said the Professor, gesturing.

And Jack sat on the strange table.

Gently, the Professor pushed Jack's shoulders down until he lay on his back. He secured Jack's wrists, legs, and torso to straps attached to the sides of the table. The Professor reached under the table and pulled a lever. The table began to rotate until Jack stood facing the audience, strapped securely to the surface.

"Professor," Jack whispered. "I can't move."

"Hush, all will be well," murmured the Professor, pulling a pointer from his coat and extending it.

"We begin by examining the mechanism's appendages, which have dexterity comparable to that of an average human being," said the Professor to his audience, his gravelly voice echoing through the hall.

The applause began again, swelling until it washed over the stage.

"Do you understand?" the Professor asked Jack, quietly.

"I do," replied Jack. "It was—I mean to say, everything that happens . . . This too, must have been written up above."

"Not in the stars, Jack," said the Professor, tapping two fingers softly against his student's temple. "Written here."

"Oh yes," said Jack. "Of course."

"Now please, sleep," said the Professor.

And Jack slept.

THE EXECUTOR

I stagger into the Executor's office just before my joint-stabilization field fails. I crumble to the floor and I can hear my nine-month-old daughter crying but my eyes aren't working for some reason. That's when I realize that I've really failed now—there's no other way to look at it.

The rest of my family is going to die, and I'm going first.

Twelve hours ago I stood in this same room on my feet, like a man. My daughter Abigail was safe and sleepy, strapped to my chest. And I still had some hope that I might save her life.

The Executor. It looms over me, imperious, an expensive hologram solid as a marble column. Flush as the devil and still with a sour mug. The machine sports the trademark scowl of the scientist who created it—my great-great-great-grandfather. The Executor has been controlling and building the family fortune for almost two hundred years. An angry old man staring down infinity with eyes like black pinpricks. Brilliant and wealthy and utterly alone, just like my ancestor.

"How much?" I ask.

"A common enough question," responds the Executor. "Trillions. Wealth that you cannot properly conceptualize. Diversified. Off-planet mining. Interworld currency exchanges. Hard mineral caches. Property. Patents. People."

"And yet your clothes are two hundred years out of date."

"Some things even I can't change, Mr. Drake. I am modeled after the original Dr. Arkady. As such, I am not allowed to . . . let's say, evolve, outside of certain constraints. My goal is to amass wealth. And my strategies toward that end are quite, ah, contemporary."

True enough. The Arkady Ransom is the largest concentration of loot on the planet. In his infamous will, Arkady made a promise that, one day, a descendant would claim the Ransom. That promise turned out to be a bucket of blood in the water. It broke my family into splinter dynasties. Sent the splinters borrowing from syndicates to pay for the Internecine War.

Arkady's promise destroyed my family.

"Lot of greenbacks," I muse. "And nobody to enjoy them."

"I certainly don't. I require no wages, Mr. Drake. No air and no light, either, for that matter. As stated in the original will and testament, *ab initio*, the profit from Dr. Arkady's investments—amassed over the last two centuries—shall be held in trust in perpetuity for the descendant who is able to claim it. So far, none has."

"A couple might have tried," I quip.

"Hundreds have tried, Mr. Drake. All have failed. Are you here to stake your claim?"

I adjust Abigail in her carrier. "For the kid," I say. "She needs a doctor. The kind that a guy like me can't even pay to consult."

"Drop her off at any state-run orphanage and they will provide for her."

"Kid's got meta-Parkinson's, like me. The state will throw her into a wheelchair and forget about her. But the disease is degenerative. It'll kill her sooner or later, unless she gets a fledgling exo-rig to build up her strength. If she can learn to walk, she could use a hybrid stepper until she's grown. Then a full-blown joint-stabilization field, just like her old man. It's real simple, Executor: I don't have enough money to save my daughter's life. You do."

The Executor looks at me, expressionless. It's tough to tell how smart it is. Those muddy eyes. The light sort of disappears into them.

"So what next?" I ask.

"The details of the review process are confidential. Touch the speaking stone to initiate."

I notice a flattish block of red sandstone on the ground.

"What else?" I ask.

"Nothing. The process begins when a legal descendant touches the stone. Once activated, the review process cannot be repeated. My decision will be final."

I cradle my daughter to my chest. She breathes in soft gasps, warm against me. My joint stabilizers whine as I kneel to touch the rock; they're army-issued and falling apart.

"Review process initiated," says the machine. "Answer the following question: What is inside you and all around you; created you and is created by you; and is you but not you?"

"It's a riddle?"

"You have five seconds to respond."

Five. Four. Three. Two. One.

As the seconds burn like match heads, my baby daughter squirms and coos. She rubs her balled up fists over her cheeks and flashes those baby blues. I focus on her and try not to think about her future. A frown flickers across the Executor's face.

Zero.

"Review process complete," says the machine. "Your claim is denied, Mr. Drake."

———

I take four numb steps toward the curb when I feel the nose of a gun jabbing into my ribs. There's nobody around, just a busy avenue buzzing with trolling auto-cars. These days, the city moves too fast for human reflexes. The streets have a numb life of their own. In turn, the citizens have become hard and precise and cold—a functioning part of the city-machine.

No drivers. No witnesses. And I've got the kid strapped to my chest.

I show my palms to the street. A slender hand clamps down on my right forearm and spins me around. A woman stares me in the face. She has a cheap-looking black polymer Beretta clutched in one gloved hand. She pauses, registers the kid sleeping against me. While her eyes are on vacation I shove the lady off balance and slap the peashooter out of her hand with a stabilizer-enhanced swipe. The lump of plastic hits the elasticrete sidewalk and I make sure it tumbles a safe distance away.

When I look up the lady has a retractable knife in her fist, coming off a tight swing. My right arm is grazed, jacket torn at the shoulder. The blade is too close to my daughter for comfort. I slow the situation down, relax my body, put my hands by my sides.

The woman's eyes shine with malice.

"Think I won't?" she asks.

"What do you need?" I ask.

"Just to give you some friendly advice, Drake," she says, motioning toward the Executor's ornate front door with the knife. "There's nothing in there for you. So don't worry about going back."

"No problem. I didn't make it through the review process anyway."

"You tried?"

"Sure I did. I'm an heir to the Arkady Ransom, aren't I?"

"Sure you did."

"That Executor is no softie. He failed me quick and didn't budge an inch. The machine's got no heartstrings to play."

She eyeballs the kid again. "Either way, it'd be a real bad idea to make a return visit. Honest, it'd be a crying shame if you got hurt. Or if somebody in your *family* got hurt—"

That's enough.

I've got her by the wrist before she can finish the sentence. I dig in with my thumb, stabilizers engaging, crushing the median nerve. Her knife drops into my other hand real neat. It's an expensive pig-sticker. High-grade nano-carbon. A steep buy, out of place on her hip.

"Say what you want to me, I got thick skin, and besides, it's probably true. But don't threaten the kid," I say.

"Bastard."

"Give me the sheath and we'll forget about it."

"You don't know who I work for," she says through gritted teeth. My thumb digs in harder. The stabilizer is rock hard and I can hear her wrist bones grinding together. She reaches back with her other hand and takes the sheath off her hip. Hands it over.

What an excellent actress. Whoever put her up to this wanted that knife to draw my attention. Well, they got what they wanted. I let go of her, sheathe the knife and slide it into my coat pocket. Abigail lets out a little mewling whine; she's starting to wake up.

The thug glares at me, rubbing her wrist. "Think you're real smart, don't you? Well I've seen smarter guys than you get dead. And then what use will you be to her?"

"Sounds like a threat. I'll bet the cops would be interested in that kind of behavior from one of their fine citizens."

The woman steps back, puffs her chest out, and laughs once. Hard.

"You don't have a clue, do you? Listen, take my advice and stay far away from here," she says, glancing at the kid. "For everybody's sake."

I head home and cram some food in the kid and change her and put her down for a nap. I make myself some lunch, eat it, clean up the sink, and then sit down at the kitchen table. I stare at the wall and listen to the auto-cars headed down to forever up on the expressway. The carbon knife sits on the table in its sheath. I pull it out and look at it: light as a feather and sharper than sunlight in space. It's got an interesting insignia pressed into it. A coat of arms.

Why'd the thug laugh when I mentioned the cops?

I sit for a while with the wooden slats of the chair pressing dents into my back, feeling the heat of the afternoon close in around me like carbon monoxide. I rub my aching right forearm stabilizer while it charges and wish I was just a little bit smarter so I could give this kid a life.

A warning. I got a warning. The lady was probably a low-level gun for hire without any solid affiliations. Could be working for anybody. Probably not the law.

I snap a pic of the coat of arms with my phone. Call it in for an image diagnostic. The ID comes back—the coat of arms reps an obscure Arkady splinter dynasty. It belongs to somebody in my family.

The Internecines have been raging since before I was born. Most people have distant cousins they run into every now and then. I have quasimilitary factions of my family that routinely wipe each other out. And all the carnage is funded by speculative investing syndicates hoping to cash in on the goldenest goose of all: the Arkady Ransom.

It makes sense that the dynasties don't want me staking a claim. The day the Arkady Ransom goes tits up will be the day the syndicates put out their hands, palms up and hungry for four generations' worth of dough. But the obvious answer doesn't feel right. That dull silver knife with its gaudy coat of arms: it screams for attention. Could be that the dynasty wants to make sure I know who I'm talking to. Or the knife's a plant and this is a frame-up job.

One thing is clear: somebody doesn't want me to figure out the Executor's riddle. But there's a soft warm lump asleep in her crib next to the kitchen window. Every troubled breath she takes is the world's best argument for figuring out the riddle. It is what it is. There's no bravery in my decision to go back. No determination or noble auspice. I've got to save my daughter for the same reason a gun has to spit bullets.

I'm a citizen of the human machine.

The phone rings and I grab it fast before it can wake up Abigail. I say hello before I realize it's a machine talking. "Attention. This is an auto-summons issued to Philip Drake." I'm to report to the police captain of the local precinct at my earliest convenience. As long as the next hour or two is convenient. Final notice.

I pick up the knife and the kid and I strap them both on.

Outside, it's one of those searing bright afternoons where the sunlight pounds into your shoulders and then comes boiling back up off the elasticrete to catch you under the chin. I hail the first auto that cruises past my house and tell it to head downtown. The air isn't working right in the vehicle so I figure out the voice command to roll down the window. I hang my arm out and curse as the red-hot door scalds me raw.

There's a bad feeling in my stomach and it's growing there like a tumor. As we pull up to the curb across from the police headquarters I see a sleek black auto switchblade into traffic.

Something doesn't feel right.

I tap a new address into my ride's keypad because I don't want to be overheard saying it out loud. Ten minutes later, we stop at a drive-thru everything store. I buy some diapers and a one-size-fits-all clip of baby food and an expensive Guardian plasma padlock.

During the drive, I play with Abigail a little. Give her my half grin and let her paw at the dimple in my cheek. It only comes out for her, now that her mother is gone.

When we reach the capsule daycare, I pick the cleanest coffin they've got and poke my head inside to make sure the lights and electrical are in order. It's a good one—most of the padding is still left on the baby-handling arm. I load the food and diaper applicators and set the entertainment to Abigail's favorite show. I give her a kiss on the face and push her inside the coffin and say good-bye. After I pay and press the door closed, it locks and seals.

Then I put the Guardian padlock on the outside, just to be sure. I kiss my fingers and press them against the glass before it goes dark for privacy.

A fist catches me in the stomach two steps into the captain's office. I get the feeling that the fist has been waiting here for me—maybe for hours, maybe for days. The knuckles are smooth and round and made of metal, attached to the assistive gripper arm of a walk-chair.

The greeting isn't entirely unexpected, but it still knocks the breath out.

Captain Bales, a gruff, bald bullet of a man, gives me a sharp nod and a nasty grin. He's a lump of muscle confined to a beat-up walk-chair that crouches on four stubby legs just inside the office door. The legged chair is gleaming and black and stripped of all branding—squat and powerful as a linebacker.

"Got your attention?" Bales asks.

He turns his back on me. The chair carries him behind a sweeping steel-top desk docked in the middle of the room like an ocean liner. Bales's broad meaty shoulders sway and tremble with each scratching step of the walk-chair.

I'm glad it was the chair that hit me and not the man.

"Pleasure to meet you, too," I wheeze, holding my stomach.

"Take a seat," he says, and I collapse into a metal slug of chair. Bales drops those meat hooks on his desk and leans forward, shoulders rising like mountains. Behind him, a wall of books looms to the ceiling, up to where only a guy with a telescoping walk-chair arm could reach.

"You got a problem, son," he says. "You made somebody very mad."

"Been known to happen," I say.

"Are you aware that the place you visited this morning is owned by a dynasty family? You were trespassing and they're not happy about it."

"Pushing it a little, aren't you?"

Bales gets very still. His brow drops and the next words come out slow and precise. "What are you talking about, Drake?"

"The dynasties don't own the Executor's office. Sure, they bought up the whole block and everything around it.

But the Executor owns its own corridor and the speaking room. It's history. First time an AI ever bought property. Maybe you ought to dust off a book or two."

"Listen, you puke, it doesn't matter who owns the corridor. You walked into the building and that whole block's owned. We got you on video breaking the law."

"This isn't about the dynasties. Who's behind it?"

"You don't ask the questions, bub. That friendly pat got you all confused."

"Fine. I'll paste in my own answers. I think it's somebody rich. Powerful. Got to be if you're here wasting your batteries bullying me. An influential somebody is worried that I'm going to hit the big score. Figure out the Ransom. Why would that be?"

"You're way off, pal."

"This isn't the first day of school for either one of us, so let's say we stop playing patty-cake like a couple of little girls?"

Bales grunts at me, leans back, and crosses his arms.

"The dynasties are a bunch of cutthroats," I say. "Criminals. They're locked in a fight that's never made an inch of progress and never will. All they do is borrow money from the syndicates and stake their failed claims and run around in tight little circles with guns. This is bigger. No planted knife is going to fool me."

Bales's face is blank. But the absence of information is plenty informational.

"Let me fill in that dull expression on your face, Captain.

The Arkady Ransom is the biggest fund on the planet. The most stable and profitable investment that's ever existed. And for one reason: it's not run by a man. It's run by a machine. A dependable, immortal, predictably successful machine. Who cares if that machine was designed by a half-crazy scientist a couple centuries ahead of his time? Who cares if I happen to be related to that man? What matters is that I've got the potential to claim the money and ruin the best investment in history. Destabilize the world economy. That's why I've got a feeling that the toes I'm stepping on belong to a government or a multinational or somebody with enough swagger to buy you a prototype McLaren walk-chair."

Bales readjusts his bulk in the legged chair.

"Great," he says. "So you're getting your little brain wrapped around it. Don't change a thing. Whoever you're dealing with, a dynasty or just a somebody, is over your head, Drake. Backing off is your only option. I could threaten you. Rough you up. God knows you think you're harder than you are. With this chair I could twist you into a goddamned pretzel and soak you in the cooler for a week. But I'm going to skip it. You're just a man and we've all got the right to wad up our lives like tissue paper and throw 'em away. My job today is just to make sure you know exactly what will happen if you go near the Executor again. You'll be throwing your life away, Drake. Walk down that road again, pal, you won't be coming back."

———

The long black auto is waiting outside. A guy who looks carved out of a rock face opens the door and motions me inside. I go because, frankly, I'm getting exhausted. Inside, the limo is as sleek and plush as the inside of a violin case—the sort you'd keep a Stradivarius in. It's also empty.

The rear wall of the limo is a curve of dark polished glass. It smells like ozone, purified air. I notice a few pinhead cameras and assume there are plenty more I can't see. The bar is all glass and light—pirate treasure glimmering just under Caribbean waves. I grab a crystal tumbler, pour myself a drink of an amber-something that could pay my rent for a month, and salute the nearest camera with it.

At that, the glass wall flickers to life and I'm looking into a three-dimensional drawing room. A man sits in a wing-back chair, staring at me with expressionless gray eyes. He's middle-aged and built slightly, but decked out in a flamboyant old-school tartan smoking jacket. No technology of any kind is visible in the room, not even a lighter. The more money a person has, the more stuff he owns that's made of real wood. And I'm guessing this fella deals in the billions. The chair he sits in, the room around him, hell, even the jacket he wears are ribbed out in exquisite patterns. It's the sort of luxurious detail that slaps you in the face with the fact that your own life is nasty, brutish, and oh so disposable. I scan the scene and sigh and then pour myself three months' rent.

Off my lack of reaction, the man finally decides to speak. "I'll get straight to the point, Drake. You're interfering.

You wouldn't listen to Bales, so I'm going to see to it that you cease. Personally."

I take a drink and savor it, feeling the buzz creeping in around the corners of my vision. The man in the glass launches two shotgun slugs of gray stare my way. My response is careful: "I'd love to take some credit for interfering, friend, but I don't know who you are."

And I'm not sure I want to.

"My name is Holland Masterson and I'll tell you who I'm not. I am not your friend. I am not your family. I am Zeus on the mountaintop. You needn't concern yourself about me except inasmuch as you should avoid incurring my wrath."

I think this over a second.

"Well, I'm glad to hear we're not related. It's families like mine that keep the callouses on gravediggers' hands."

"You refer to the Internecines. Pathetic. A broken family borrowing money and making promises to strangers so they can arm themselves to murder each other. The late Dr. Arkady had amazing prescience to build the Executor. He knew the calculating avarice of so-called family and he sought to avoid it."

A trace of anger ripples over the man's face. It's like spotting a shark fin out of the corner of your eye. Something's hidden under the surface here. Something with teeth.

"I take it you're not a family man?"

"I am not, Mr. Drake. I believe achievement is the only measure of a man. And each man will be measured on his own before the eyes of God. Everything I have accomplished was achieved on my own merits. Only *I* taste the fruit of those labors."

"So what do you leave behind when you're gone?"

"A legacy of triumph. And preferably, as small a gang of squabbling vultures as is possible. Think of the pharaohs, Mr. Drake. They left behind pyramids to shine brightly through the ages. Their descendants fell into madness and despair long before time could ravage the beauty of those monuments."

"Sounds lonely as hell in there."

Masterson shoots those gray bullets at me again. Then the padded shoulders slump. "You are not the best version of yourself and thus you cannot understand. You are only capable of taking commands. Very well, do not approach the Executor. Do not ask why. And do not interfere with me again or you will learn what pain feels like."

The screen fades back to dark polished glass and I notice the auto isn't moving anymore. For a second, I'm staring into my own flat, faded reflection. My face looks wooden and blank—a goddamned toy soldier on the march, drink in hand.

Then a shadow falls across the window and the driver yanks open the door with a *thunk*. Blinking at the sudden blazing sunlight, I step out of perfumed ozone and into hot reality. I don't hear the driver slam the door shut. I'm busy grasping the fact that I'm standing in front of the capsule daycare—the word *pain* still ringing in my ears.

The Guardian plasma lock is sliced, lying on the ground next to the capsule. I pick it up and the dribble of melted metal is still warm from whatever industrial torch ate through it. With shaking fingers, I drop the privacy screen and unlock the capsule.

Inside, Abigail is lying on her back, watching the vidscreen with one eye and working on putting her foot into her mouth. She's fine and dandy—a cog in this efficient coffin-shaped machine. I exhale and then take a deep breath, realizing that I've been gut punched since I saw the lock on the ground. Message received, Mr. Masterson.

But some things you can't change.

I sit on the curb outside the capsule daycare with Abigail on my lap and watch the street for an older-model auto. The old ones are made of metal instead of plastic, and they cost less. I hail the first likely suspect and direct it to stop off at a Japanophile store. There, I drop the last of my cash on a portable impact shell. The hot pink pod is hard outside and padded inside—gyro-stabilized and designed to keep an infant safe at ultrahigh speeds. Hard to believe that in some places there's no stigma attached to taking your baby on a turbo-bike.

I shrug the shell onto my chest and slide Abigail into it. She's like a chubby pearl inside a clam. The glistening hull is rated for everything from impact to puncture to temperature and pressure fluctuations. With a couple of sharp yanks, I secure the impact shell to my chest, straps cutting into my shoulders. Then I close the breather lid on top and listen for the gyros to engage. A soothing blue light spreads across the top of the shell, forming a happy face. Very Japanese.

The auto waits for us patiently, like a dog. An upgrade job, it has a vestigial driver compartment with a steering wheel and everything. The auto is doing its part in this clockwork city. All of us are doing our part. Not because we want to or even because we have to, but because it's the only way there is. You don't pick where the highway goes, you just keep one eye on the horizon and hope you're headed someplace nice.

I peek into the driver's-side window and notice a layer of dust on the front seat. The hunk of metal was never designed for this, but all of us have got to adapt. I drum my fingers on the roof and sigh, then grab the door handle and yank it open. I crawl inside the doomed auto and buckle myself in and roll down the windows so the glass won't cut me when it shatters.

There are more suits outside the offices than I expected. I catch at least one with the first jump over the curb. He has a confused look on his face and a gun in his hand for a split second. Then he is gone. Under the auto somewhere or maybe he dove out of the way.

Nobody ever drives an auto on manual anymore—surprise.

The rest of the lookouts scatter as a ton of screeching metal gallops over the curb and plows into the front door of the Executor's office. The safety belt catches me hard, dislocating my shoulder. A spray of red light slashes my face and the impact shell emits a warning shriek. The front door of the building explodes, spraying splinters into the dark corridor leading to the Executor's office.

It's quiet for an ear-ringing five seconds after impact. Dust from the pulverized office door floats in my open windows. I glance down at my chest and see a bright red sad face on top of the impact shell, fading back to a safe blue.

Breathing in ragged gasps, I try to unclip my safety belt and hiss in pain. I wrap my good arm around my hurt shoulder, hold my breath, and ram the auto door a couple times. The joint pops back into the socket and I'm underwater for a second with my pain. Tires screech and men shout as other autos arrive.

"It's Drake!" shouts somebody.

I kick the dented door open and clamber over the hood of the auto, stepping through the splintered door frame into the dark corridor. At the end of the hallway, I draw my piece and turn back to aim it at the crashed auto wedged into a rectangle of fading evening light. A dark face peeks in but disappears quick when it sees me coiled up in the shadows like a viper.

One hand over my baby, I squeeze the trigger until I see a ball of fire.

I stagger just inside the door to the Executor's office before my joint-stabilization field fails. I crumble to the floor and I can hear Abigail crying but my eyes aren't working for some reason. I try to hug the impact shell tight against me but my arms won't listen to my brain.

An explosion rocks the hallway on the other side of the door.

I realize that I've really failed now. It was always a long shot. Strong out of the gate but faded on the stretch. In the end, no threat.

Then, the shell gives off a soft blue glow.

My eyes still work. It must be dark because they've cut the power to the building. My joint stabilizers failed, but now they've flipped to local batteries instead of leeching the ambient power supply. The stabilizers quiver—they're having trouble pulling out a pattern to offset the noise coming from my diseased nervous system.

I'm able to drag myself into a sitting position and flip the lid on the impact shell. Abigail is inside, angry and fussing but not hurt. And of course, looming over me, watching without expression, is the Executor. The ghost of the old man himself, standing in the blue-tinged darkness.

"Why didn't you listen to Mr. Masterson?" asks the machine.

"Who?" I ask. "The spook?"

That gives the Executor a pause.

"To what are you referring?" it asks.

I drag myself onto my feet, using the wall. "I'm referring to the fact that Holland Masterson was nothing but a
hologram, cooked up by another hologram. The only one
I know. You."

I make sure the door is locked. As secure as it's going
to get.

"And what made you aware of this fact?"

"Choice of subject, pal. A legacy of triumph? I'm no
genius. But that's a conversation I could have had with old
man Arkady two hundred years ago. That and the decor in
Masterson's little drawing room. Out of date. Some things
even you can't change, right?"

"Correct."

"How long have you been doing this, Executor? Playing
my family off each other?"

"Why, ever since I was created, I suppose."

"You tried too hard. That's what gave it away. If you
weren't worried, you wouldn't have tried so hard. And I
figured out why."

"Please enlighten me," says the machine, eyes half-lidded,
confident. A distant thud rocks the building. I figure this
means they've reparked my auto. Won't be long before this
room is flooded with very angry men.

I don't say anything to the Executor. Favoring my busted
shoulder, I pull Abigail out of the impact shell. She is small
and warm and squirming in her pajamas. She's been crying.
I wipe her face with my shirtsleeve and set her gently down

on the speaking stone. The Executor drops the confident act and stares, eyes glittering like beetles.

"When a legal descendant touches the stone," I say, "the process begins."

With that reminder, the Executor's automatic behavior kicks in like the last second of a magic trick. "Review process initiated," it says. "Answer the following question: What is inside you and all around you; created you and is created by you; is you but not you?"

"Your answer is sitting right here," I say.

On all fours, Abigail cranes her neck to look up at me. She gives me a slobbery grin and tries to reach for me. I give her back half a smile and my index finger and then I throw a glance at the Executor.

"Family," I say. "The answer to your riddle is *family*. Old man Arkady never had one, really. Maybe that's why he booby-trapped the lives of everyone who came after him. Started the Internecines by creating you and keeping his wealth around forever, like poisoned bait. He was brilliant and maybe more machine than man and he didn't realize what was important until it was too late. You were the closest thing the old man ever had to family, sad and pathetic and wrong as that may be. Family is what he feared most. Family is what he always wanted but never had."

The Executor is silent for a few seconds.

"Claim approved," it says. "Until Miss Abigail Drake is of age, the Arkady estate will be held in abeyance. Upon her aetatis suae eighteen, all goods and chattels shall be conveyed to her as sole inheritor. However, at this time you have no claim to the monies—"

"I'm not after your money, pal."

"Very well, then—"

"But I've got one more thing to say to you. So listen close."

The Executor stands very still, watching me like a predator.

"As her guardian," I say, "*you're* part of her family now. And if you are called upon, my friend, you will give her a life not imaginable to a person like me. A life of wealth and travel. Knowledge. You'll protect her. You'll bend every twisted circuit of your will to guide her, to help make her a strong and good and just woman. And in due time, she will become the matriarch of our line and your successor. When that day comes you will step down, Executor. And Abigail Drake will carry on our family name in peace. Understand?"

"Yes, Mr. Drake. I understand."

"Good," I say, ignoring a foreboding rumbling coming from the hallway. "Now I've got to go out there and settle this before they come in here and settle it for us."

"Are you sure that's safe?"

"It's as safe as anything."

"I'm afraid they've cut off my communications. I'm not able to cancel my previous orders. However, the police will arrive in less than four minutes—"

The machine is cut off as something big and loud happens just outside. But I'm not watching the machine. I'm putting Abigail back inside the impact shell. I tuck her in and set the shell on the speaking stone with the lid open.

"We don't have four minutes. If they get in here, they'll shoot everything that moves."

"I'll simply talk to them, order them to stop."

"I don't think that's going to help much, friend. I made a messy entrance. They're understandably upset."

I check my revolver and holster it under my left arm. The knife I secure in the waistband of my pants, in the small of my back. I juice my stabilizers to full power, until my arms and legs hum with strength. Should last about five minutes. Plenty long enough.

Only then do I allow myself one last look. The pink shell rests on the stone. Inside it, the world's wealthiest individual is blowing spit bubbles at me. I press my sagging holster against my chest so the gun won't bump her and lean down and kiss Abigail on her forehead. I close my eyes for a second, just a blink, and inhale her smell. Her skin is soft as rose petals on my stubbled chin and I remind myself to try and remember this detail for later—for when things get bad.

Somehow, later is always closer than you think.

I close the impact shell and stride over to the quivering door. With one hand I check the knife again to make sure I can draw it fast. I give the machine a stern look but the Executor knows the score.

I grab hold of the doorknob and put my head down. Take a breath. Flex my arms until the joint stabilizers are singing.

"You're a good father," says the Executor.

I hear the thugs in the hall outside, shuffling past each other, body armor clinking. I feel a cold spot on my chest where my daughter is missing. I know that each of us has to do our part in this city, like clockwork.

"No, I'm not," I say to the Executor. "But you better be."

And I step through the door.

HELMET

My little brother Chima sleeps with his mouth open. He has for a long time, not that he's got a choice. He was seven years old when the Helmet caught me off guard. A corrugated metal wall exploded and hot shrapnel tore through Chima's face. Fuel-accelerated flames ate his cheeks and mouth. Only my brother's wide, round eyes were left untouched, glittering with intelligence behind a mask of flash-welded flesh.

The Helmets. Those baby killers. They always come at dawn.

Heat hits the Ukuta fast in the morning. Rays of sunlight

splinter the horizon and needle into the slums. The sterile kilometers around our sprawling shantytown, where the old radiation lives—those hills dance and sing and remain still at the same time. And our valley of trash, with its labyrinth of crumbling walls and shacks and dirt paths, is trapped, groaning under the weight of that great wavering lump of heat. The sun beats down upon us as if it bears a grudge. Like it was angry at us for our very existence.

In Ukuta, you see, we must defy men and gods to live.

The election cycles come four times a year. Our votes are our own. But a careless vote can make the gray hills dance with more than heat. A wink of light from golden armor. The Helmets. Always a team of two. Vaulting through the dead wastes that have long divorced Ukuta from a place once called Africa. Those shivering hills will not suffer life to pass, but the Helmets bound through it unheeded, immune to the ancient poison.

Crossing the veil of death to guide us.

The Triumvirate rules the city-state of Ukuta. Their propaganda flyers drop from the sky, fluttering down like dying sparrows. During the night, images appear painted on walls. In the morning, we fear to remove them. Always the same image: Three old men, squatting like vultures behind a soaring judge's bench. Three wrinkled faces scowling down at us. "Follow our guidance," command the signs.

Without words, the Helmets appear and show us the strength of the Triumvirate. We do not question the filthy water or the smoke-filled factories or the invisible ring of death that surrounds Ukuta. Violence guides our vote. The faceless Helmets stamp out our phantom uprisings before we realize they have begun.

Chima stops breathing. I count to four before the rangy twelve-year-old snorts. He wakes up scrabbling at the plastic tarp he uses for a blanket.

It is early and he does not yet have his rag over his face. His pink hole of a mouth gapes like a rotten tree hollow. Rubbing his eyes, he frantically scans the miles of shanties that climb the horizon. He runs his fingertips over his face and moans at me in alarm.

"Ajani," he says, and I see the glint of shrapnel embedded in his cheeks. I have to concentrate to make out the words hidden inside his grunting whimper.

"My face hurts," he says.

My pulse quickens. Sometimes, when the Helmets are near, the shards of metal buried in Chima's face come alive with pain. The boy told me the aching comes from the silent talking between the Helmets. He says it is their radio antennae. I do not understand this, but Chima is a very clever boy. When his face hurts, especially at dawn, it can only mean one thing: we are in danger.

Standing, I put a hand to our chalky cement wall and listen. The world is still this early. Distantly, someone coughs and hawks phlegm. Two women talk quietly, headed to the well with empty plastic jugs. One of them carries a pocket radio in her hand, quietly squawking drum-laced music. Chima winces as the radio grows nearer and then recedes.

"Radio," he says.

I take a relieved breath.

Then, I feel a vibration. Followed by a twin vibration one second later.

Chima sees it in my face before I can speak. He scrambles out of his cardboard bed and crawls through the refuse toward our one solid wall. There is a hole carved in the base of it that he still fits inside. He disappears, curling into the gap, knees to his chest and head folded down.

"I will tell you when it is safe," I say, picking up a stubby spear fashioned out of a stake of sharpened rebar. The handle is made of plastic that has been melted onto the shaft and then wrapped in twine and cardboard. It fits the groove of my fingers perfectly.

Others are starting to stir. It won't be long before the panic spreads. Today, the shanties will burn.

I reach into the cool hollow and touch Chima on his bony shoulder to reassure him. Give him a grin and a wink. Then I prop his bedding loosely over the hole. Smack the supports out from under our makeshift roof and let the warped plastic shield fall against this one good wall, draping itself over my brother's hiding spot. Going around the side, I climb the wall's broken tail. I balance on top and squint at the horizon.

Two Helmets advance down the distant hill. They are man-shaped, but made of metal armor. They bound ahead, sometimes half a kilometer at a leap, leaving behind swollen mushrooms of fire with their flame-makers. That which isn't concrete burns. Wood and plastic and paper turn to ash. As does flesh.

Especially flesh.

Concrete walls are our only oasis. I fought for this half-demolished wall I am perched on. Memory of the fight is in the weal of knotted scar tissue that arcs down my chest. Even now, those slum dwellers who dart past below see my spear and they know better than to make a challenge.

The Helmets' direction is hard to gauge, but their silhouettes are growing larger.

I drop flat onto my stomach, hugging the wall. More runners are heading this way down the hill. They flee like rabbits, blindly. There are more ways to die than the flame. Breaking a bone or ripping your flesh are invitations to meet death. The wise among us have prepared hiding holes. Our fortresses to defend.

My breath comes in even and slow. My eyes do not blink. Sweat tickles my brow. I wipe it away, and then my breath catches. I have lost sight of the lead Helmet. I crane my neck, and that fat old bastard in the sky beats down on my eyes, blinding me. A flicker of shadow crosses my face, and the earth lurches.

I cling to my wall, spear held tight.

The Helmet has arrived. It stands in the alley, six feet tall and sheathed in iridescent plates of armor. As the Helmet walks, each elaborate metal sheath flexes with its own mind. Its limbs move like an insect, in a series of sudden precise gestures. The Helmet inspects the area with quick jerks of its head. When it turns its gaze on me, I see it does not have a face.

Just the gold sheen of a reflective visor.

I lie still and feel the grit of my wall stinging my flesh. If the machine takes another step closer, I will try and kill it. To attack is a death sentence. I know this. But I have let my brother down once before. And I will never let Chima be hurt again, no matter what.

The Helmet steps into our clearing and lifts its flame-maker.

In one fluid twisting movement, I fall from the wall and use the momentum to sling my arm. The spear flies true, tassel fluttering behind it. It strikes the Helmet in the faceplate and bounces away, leaving a wicked crack snaking across the golden visor. The Helmet does not react.

I have failed to kill it, and now my own life is forfeit.

I circle slowly around, leading the Helmet away from my brother. I see my reflection in the thing's visor, my face shining and split. The thing leaps and closes the twenty feet between us. It clamps a hand over my forearm. Holds me with the dead final weight of a fallen tree.

Faintly, I think I hear someone screaming. From far away.

With all my strength, I resist looking back at my wall, resist checking on my little brother. If he is not roasted alive, he will likely survive. He is resourceful and doesn't eat much. After I am dead, those few people who remember the young face that used to grin beneath his eyes will watch out for him.

The Helmet lifts me high and I hang by my savaged wrist, watching my own hazy reflection. Gold-sheathed fingers grab me and I am thrown over the Helmet's shoulder. An arm lowers and presses me into place. Metal shoulder plates writhe under my belly. The Helmet does not kill me.

Instead, it carries me away.

Just before the Helmet leaps, I catch sight of Chima, watching with angry, tear-filled eyes from behind our wall. I shake my head and he stays hidden.

The sun glares murderously through a barricade of clouds. I can almost picture heaven above the glowing haze. But I know it's a nightmare of raging light.

I lose consciousness somewhere over the dancing hills. My face blisters with the cold heat rising off the poisoned land. I do not think to struggle. The world is too bright, white on white on white. The Helmet's skin bites my side with every movement. My strength is gone. I flop like a rag doll.

When I wake, I do not recognize this place. I have never been outside Ukuta. No slum dweller has.

Tall blank buildings loom under low dirty clouds. The Helmet carries me down a narrow street, its walls crowding in. The gray surfaces are sprinkled with rain, gleaming dull and strong in the cloud-diffused sunlight. My mind balks to imagine it. In Ukuta, each of these walls would be worth fighting for. They make my humpbacked wall seem grotesque and sad in comparison.

"Helmet," I gasp. "Where are you taking me?"

The Helmet does not react in any way. No pause, no glance, no small nod of the head. We continue walking, the Helmet's armored boots clinking off the empty street. The staccato sound plinks off the walls with the regularity of a metronome. Like a clock ticking down the seconds of my life. Until it stops.

The wall beside us is studded with coffin-sized, rectangular doors.

A bronze carving of a helmet rests in the center of each door. A bronze handle emerges from the mouth-section of the carving. The Helmet reaches out and locks gauntleted fingers to the handle. With a prehistoric groan, the Helmet flexes its armored might and drags a shining metal slab from the wall. It takes a long time to pull it all the way out. Finally, the slab of metal hangs there fully extended, like a tombstone.

The Helmet throws me onto the slab and I am too exhausted to resist.

I count my breaths as the Helmet pushes the grinding slab back into the wall with me on it. Arms by my sides, the ceiling of the tomb nearly scrapes my bare heaving chest. Darkness eats my body, and inch by inch, my face sinks into blackness. My breath echoes in my ears.

Buried alive.

For ten breaths, I lie in the darkness unable to move. My palms are flat against the cold sweating metal, pushing, fingers splayed. I try to crane my neck and a chilly dot of ceiling presses against my forehead. A humming vibration swells around me, inside me.

The ceiling explodes into light. Things I have never seen before streak overhead, numbers and letters and images. My eyelashes pulse with their blue glow. Then an outline of my own body hovers overhead, a mirror reflection. I pant faster, breathing my own carbon dioxide.

The slab beneath me is heating up.

Overhead, the stark blue outline of my body is starting to turn red around the edges. I spread my fingers and scream out in pain as my thumb is burned. Quickly, I realize that I've got to match my body to the outline. The red is pain, and it is closing in. Hunching my whole body, I shuffle to match the silhouette. I whimper once, when the heel of my foot strays into fire.

The tomb whines mechanically, begins to shiver.

I blink away tears of pain and focus on the image. Sweat is pooling in the hollow of my throat. I can feel beads of it tickling my ribs and thighs and calves. But the pain of disobeying is so intense that I have no choice.

The lights above me blink out.

In the darkness, the warm metal around me begins to rise up like dough. The sudden overwhelming heat of it crushes the breath out of my lungs in a silent gasping scream. Before I can take another breath, the metal is over me, burying me, rising up around my neck like crushing water. A finger of liquid metal pokes into my belly, piercing my skin. If I could scream or kick or struggle I would.

Instead, I lie paralyzed, drowning in this cube of space as my taut, bony body is swallowed by flowing metal.

I try to breathe in and I cannot. I try to move and I cannot. I try to live, but I cannot.

The Helmet is my living tomb.

Cooling metal encases every inch of my body with cascading sheaths that flex and coil like a python. Only the surface of my face does not touch metal. Inside the Helmet, I am free to curl my lips in anguish and scream into the two inches of space between my eyes and the visor.

And scream I do.

The Helmet holds me fast. I cannot move anything. Not a finger. I am trapped inside a human-shaped prison cell. The horror is not that I cannot move. The horror is that the Helmet moves itself, and me with it.

The machine bends its knees and stands up. Struggling, I flex against its movements. I grunt and curse and whimper, throwing every ounce of strength into resisting the will of the machine. But metal is stronger than flesh. The Helmet mechanically forces my limbs into position.

After only thirty seconds I am too tired to resist.

Beaten, I watch through the visor as my body slides off the slab. Walking down the narrow street, I realize I can hear my clinking footsteps on the pavement. A speaker inside the Helmet is transmitting sound from outside.

Another Helmet approaches from the other direction.

We do not pause or acknowledge each other in any way. In its visor, I see the gleaming reddish armor that has replaced my skin.

We both turn to enter a squat cement building. Inside, rows of narrow corridors stretch beneath a crushingly low ceiling. Each row is illuminated every few feet by a flickering overhead light. And in each row stand hundreds of identical Helmets, each a precise distance from the other, postures identical. Their faces are only inches from the wall.

In a rush of sickening horror, it dawns on me that every Helmet has a person trapped inside. I wonder how many of them are screaming right now, struggling against unstoppable metal. My Helmet walks me down the row. Only now do I notice subtle differences in the Helmets' armor, nicks and scars. Faded patches and burned spots. And some of the Helmets are shorter than others.

Those must be the women.

I walk past a shorter Helmet and take an empty space at the wall. I only glimpse at the girl next to me for an instant. I assume she is a girl, anyway. She is very small. Her armor is finer than mine, intricately layered together and burnished orange.

"Doli," I say to myself. "She is like a doll."

My voice echoes loudly inside the Helmet. Somehow it is reassuring. A relief to know that, even if I cannot make a fist, at least my voice is my own, however silent it may be to those outside.

My stomach cramps and I groan. Spasms rip through my

gut and I want to fall and curl up in a ball. But the Helmet stands firm. Rolling my eyes, I make out an umbilical arm reaching out from the wall. It must be connected to a port on my stomach. Delivering sustenance. Removing waste.

The Helmets are feeding.

I begin to silently cry. The wall before me is flat and empty and huge in my visor. It is made of cold hard cement. A spiderweb of tiny fissures runs through it. Nothing changes. Nothing moves. After a few moments, the wall loses perspective. I feel as though I am looking down at a map. Each crack is a wall back home in Ukuta. I can imagine Chima sleeping safely. Thousands of other villagers around him. He can hear the barking of a far-off dog. The cool night breathes on his skin.

My crying stops.

One by one, the overhead lights snap out. The wall before me drops a shade darker with each *snap* of the light. *Snap, snap, snap.* It is the only sound until finally we Helmets stand together in twilight. Utterly alone in our multitudes.

"Chima," I say it out loud and it feels good. "Good night, brother."

My own walking wakes me.

Instead of the wall, my visor displays a long tunnel. The passage is the width of a single man, the ceiling but a few inches overhead. The short Helmet, Doli, marches ahead of me. Others are in front of her. I imagine still more are behind me, but I cannot turn to look. Staring hard at Doli, I think I catch a trace of femininity in the way she walks.

And the tunnel disappears. Opens up into a huge empty room. Cement floors lit by a skylight, glowing with smoky sunlight. A thousand Helmets stand in sweeping formation, meticulously spaced. As I march into my own position, I realize that we are all oriented to face one point.

A towering judge's bench across the room, made of ancient wood. Three wrinkled, scowling faces peek over the top. I recognize the Triumvirate.

In the propaganda posters, these men always seemed identical. But standing before them, I see the First has a sharp nose and birdlike eyes. He hunches forward, his great bald head hanging between narrow shoulders. The Second is ancient. Age spots mottle his brow and his thin shaking fists are visible. The Third is a piggish monster. He licks his moist lips and stares down at us through a wet sneer. His face is nearly lost in the waddle of flesh around his neck.

The man-things speak together, finishing each other's sentences. A three-headed monster perched at the top of a wooden wall.

"War criminals," says the First, shrilly.

"Are you not ashamed?" howls the Second.

"Murderers, know that your path leads to death," mutters the Third, with a shapeless lisp.

Standing at attention, arms by my sides, I can only swivel my eyes to witness the rage-filled faces. They deliver their speech by rote, as they will every morning from now on.

"Your grisly work benefits the Triumvirate. Your wicked deeds further the Cause. Yet we sit apart from your crimes. For you are not innocent," spits the First.

"Criminals responsible for atrocity," says the Second.

"Killers, poisoners, usurpers," mutters the Third.

"You have turned your hand to evil deeds. And you will be punished with death," says the Second.

"When your term expires, so must you," adds the Third, staring blindly.

The First continues, intoning the words like a prayer: "The responsibility for what you have done sweeps through your metal skin like a foul wind through the branches of the tree of death. It sinks its barbs into your flesh. And it will be set free by the purifying flame upon your skin."

"For the wages of sin . . . ," intones the Third.

"Death," they say together, solemnly. "Death. Death."

In my peripheral, I see six Helmets draw their flame-makers and walk forward. The rest of us reorient our faces to follow. The six walking Helmets have chipped armor. Their visors are dimmed and faded with sunlight. Forming into three pairs, they stop at the base of the wall and raise their weapons to each other. No hesitation. Flames spurt out, coating each Helmet in an inferno. The golden metal shells stand firm, each continuing to pull the trigger.

The Helmets burn.

Finally, one falls to its knees. Still, it keeps flaming its partner. Another falls, and another. Mercifully, it ends. The chemical flames gutter and evaporate into nothing. Six charred Helmets lie on the ground, frozen in their last positions, visors stained black with soot.

By some twisted logic, we are being punished for the Helmets' crimes.

I wonder how long the people inside lived. I wonder if they were even alive when they entered the room. Were they scared in those last moments? Or maybe they were relieved. Some part of me senses that the execution was merciful.

We Helmets. Baby killers. We always come at dawn.

I can only observe, locked in my shell. Through my visor I see there are many slums beyond Ukuta. Each area is isolated by a dead zone of old radiation. These tracts of land keep the people separated and weak. Ignorant of each other, the slums vote constantly, always reaffirming the control of the Triumvirate.

My Helmet guides me, and the Triumvirate guides the people.

Our raids are conducted in pairs. Little Doli is my permanent companion. Short and squat, she is nonetheless powerful. I have seen the streak of her burnt orange armor arcing high above the nameless, faceless slums. A twinkling morning star, she falls through the sky trailing a jet of cleansing flame.

The days come and go as a waking nightmare. Weeks pass in which I cannot bear to open my eyes. I feel the lurch of my body as it leaps through the dead zones. The disturbing tickle of radiation seeps through the armor. The inevitable sound of Doli, always a few seconds behind me. My faithful echo. I hear the desperate curses of our victims. Their lamentations. Their begging.

And in the end, their silence.

I accumulate sin. Cement crumbles beneath my boots. My gauntleted fingers rend flesh. Flames spew from my weapon and then speak to me in guttural whispers as they eat their fill of innocent flesh.

My lips are the only thing I can control.

"Good morning, Doli," I say at the feeding station. "Did you sleep well, my dear? Of course you did, how could you not?"

Together, Doli and I stream out of the city, along with a thousand other Helmets. We break into a steady trot and I begin to talk. I know that Doli cannot hear me, but I leave in the pauses and imagine her responses.

"Doli, do you want to hear a story?" I ask.

I suppose.

"Did I ever tell you the one about how Chima claimed our wall?"

Only a hundred times.

"The Ajani wall, as it came to be known, was controlled by a fat brute called Cleaver."

Why'd they call him Cleaver?

"He was dangerous enough with his weapon to be named after it. No way to get near his wall. But it was the finest, safest wall in all of Ukuta."

How did little Chima claim it?

"My brother Chima searched far and wide to find a butcher in need of a cleaver. Told him about this perfect knife. That butcher came one day and traded Cleaver a whole goat for his weapon."

Uh-oh.

"That's right, Doli. Without his legendary knife, fat old Cleaver had no chance to defend his wall. I took it away from him with only a single wound. A clever boy, that Chima. Much smarter than his older brother, that's for sure."

We are leaping, soaring over yet another dead zone.

When we touch down, the slum looks like any other. The screams are the same. The crackle of flames.

I almost do not recognize the stick-thin boy running at me. His eyes burn with evil and hatred. As the rag covering his face falls away, I see the pink smear of flesh that is his face and recognize my own brother.

"Chima," I say. Or maybe I only think his name.

My head rings with the impact of metal on metal. Chima has set a trap. Our wall surges into my vision just before it collapses onto me. The disintegrating rock smashes into my body, pulls me down in a wave of rubble. As the pain of the reverberation lances through my head, I pray for my prison to shatter, to fracture and fall away like plaster. I pray for Chima to be victorious. I pray for my own death.

But the strength of the Helmet will not succumb to prayer.

The armor is intact. I feel my arm questing through the

broken shards. A slab of powdery cement scrapes off my visor and falls away. I sit up from the bed of sharp rock. Chima falls upon me, vicious, swinging my old rebar spear.

"Die, demon," he screams, each word a guttural cough. "Why won't you die?"

He is too close. My Helmet grabs Chima with one hand. Pulls him toward me and slams him onto his back. I hear his ribs snapping against the uneven rubble. Yet he continues to roar.

A warrior.

I choke down tears as my armored fingers crush my brother's throat. Blinking, I focus on his face. This sweet boy whom I raised and protected for so many years. When he screams, I bite through my own lips and scream with him.

"I love you, Chima," I sputter.

I cannot close my eyes to the horrible sight.

The one I love more than myself is dying inches from me. Suffocating with a broken neck. And all I can do is greedily memorize his features. Each fleck of shrapnel in his cheeks. His smoke-black eyes. Thick, arched eyebrows, twisted in venomous anger. In a moment, my body will leap away empty-handed. These memories will be all that I can carry.

The life leaves his eyes and I feel it leave my own, as well. My little brother chokes, chest heaving, and his jaw moves. Mouths a final word.

Ajani.

It is not until later that I receive Chima's gift.

He found the answer in the shrapnel embedded in his face. Said it hurt him because of the radio transmissions between Helmets. And my Chima recognized a weak spot. Where there is radio, he must have thought, there is an antenna. Destroy the antenna and the radio cannot function.

Such a clever boy.

Our beautiful wall fell and pinned my Helmet in its ruin. Brave as a lion, Chima struck again and again. His blows were not random. Each landed in one spot at the base of my spine. The armored lump resting there was damaged, but not destroyed. Not yet.

It happens while I'm crossing the dancing hills, the familiar nibble of radiation in my legs. I am midleap when I feel something wrong. I open my eyes and notice the ground is coming too fast. My Helmet is not reacting. Instinctively, I try to thrust out my hands before I hit the poisoned dirt and rock.

I smash into the toxic hardpack like a meteorite.

Rolling, limbs flailing, rocks battering my ribs and head—I luxuriate in the pain. Each gasp is a wonder, a reminder that I am still alive inside this cage. My own arms and legs are weak as dead grass but the Helmet is amplifying my tiniest movements. Climbing to my knees, I feel the venomous heat pouring up out of the ground and into my face. Sweat drips from my forehead and streaks the inside of my visor. The orange flash of Doli is rapidly disappearing ahead. Only enemies wait behind me.

My wall is gone. My brother gone.

I scramble to my feet and make a clumsy leap after Doli. My powered legs catapult my body into the air. It is a jerky, mechanical leap that sends me cutting through the sky like a bullet. There is no feel of wind on my face, no roar of the air in my ears. Even so, I find that for the first time I enjoy the leap.

As we near the walled city, other incoming Helmets join us. It takes all of my concentration to maintain the scripted movements that my body has repeated day after day: Form in a line outside the city. March through the gate. Down narrow alleys. Every nerve in my body is pleading, begging for me to run away. Rip this Helmet off my flesh. Feel the air on my skin.

But Doli marches ahead of me. Her frame is so small. Armor beginning to flake from our constant trips through the dancing hills. She is trapped, just as I was. Just as all Helmets are.

And I cannot abandon her.

On schedule, we enter the feeding tunnel. I march in careful step until I reach my hole in the wall. I stand the right distance away from Doli, face the wall, and draw on every last shred of my willpower to keep my superpowered limbs perfectly still. That cursed umbilical tube emerges and my stomach spasms as the blind, grasping appendage delivers sustenance and removes waste.

Snap, snap, snap.

The overhead lights blink out. We are left in semidarkness, an endless row of shadowed statues standing at attention. No movement, no sound. Except the quiet, oh so quiet, grind of my Helmet.

I turn my head slightly to the left, to see Doli. Nothing happens. No alarm sounds.

In this world of sameness, I am miraculously different. A sculpted man come to life and alone in the company of my fellow works of art. I gingerly reach up and take my Helmet in both hands. My fingers are so strong; I must be careful. Gently, I pull my visor straight up.

Metal strains. The visor hisses at the neck as the first rip appears. The helmet comes unmarried from the armor.

And finally, blissfully, cool air washes over my filthy face.

Smells. I can smell wet concrete around me. The strange chemical smell from the umbilical devices. My own breath and hair and skin take on a long-forgotten stink in contrast to these new odors. I sniff deeply and nearly cry out from the joy of air rushing into my nostrils. My tears evaporate from my cheeks and the feeling is blessed. Finally, I remember Doli.

She stands loyally next to me, as always, facing her wall.

I place a hand on her shoulder. In all the massacres and slaughter, our Helmets have never touched. I don't even really know that she is a she. It could be anyone in there. Leaning over, I look into her visor. In the reflection, I see my lips are flecked with blood, lost in a tightly curled beard, and my cheeks streaked with sweat. I notice that I am smiling, my teeth yellow and bright in the darkened corridor.

"I have been looking forward to meeting you for a long time, Doli," I whisper. "You do not know this, but we have had many conversations. We are old friends."

What must she be thinking? This change in routine. To be on the cusp of freedom after so long. Countless years of bloodshed and evil and those frowning monsters shouting down accusations of sin and responsibility.

With both hands, I take hold of her helmet.

Squeezing, I gently pull the visor up. A seam appears at the neck. Squealing, the metal parts. A putrid stench spews from the gap. I retch once before I can hold my breath. In a last burst, I tear the visor off. Stumbling backward, gasping for air, I finally meet Doli.

She is a she.

At first, I think Doli is smiling at me. And then I realize that she has no lips. Her teeth are bared at me in a rictus of pain and insanity. She has chewed through her own mouth and swallowed most of it and done the same for large pieces of her tongue. It has healed and been eaten again. Bits of rotting flesh line the inside of her visor. Blood and vomit and saliva coat the interior of her visor, obscuring the view.

I realize it is possible that Doli has never even seen me.

Clumps of hair cling to her peeling scalp. A stiff strand is plastered over one of her eyes. She has had no way to move it, maybe for years. Her eyes roll idiotically in their sockets. She moans, and I think of my murdered brother.

"I'm so sorry, Doli," I say.

With all the gentleness I can muster, I push the crusted hair out of her eyes. Smooth it back in an uneven mass behind her ears. Then, reverently, I fit her visor back over her head. I press it down hard, crushing the metal seal back together. Then, I do the same for myself. Turn and face my own patch of nothing.

I leave Doli there, small, facing the blank wall.

The Triumvirate guides us.

The three man-things huddle together behind the towering wooden wall of their bench. Twisted faces peering down from above. But I have leapt higher in my months-long orgy of murder. I have vaulted city walls and crushed huddling families to ruin under my boots. Brushed my fingers over the throats of men and left yawning corpses. I have heard wild flames licking the bodies of the fallen.

We thousand Helmets stand at attention in a sweeping semicircle, arms by our sides, facing the bench, a mute audience held captive. Forced to absorb blame and abuse and madness. Each of us a slave to his own machine.

All save one.

As they do every morning, the Triumvirate speaks together, finishing each other's sentences. The three-headed monster is here on schedule to lay down its sins upon our strong shoulders.

"War criminals," says the First, voice booming.

"Are you not ashamed?" howls the Second.

"Murderers, know that your path leads to death," mutters the Third.

And I take a step forward.

"Your grisly work . . . ," says the First, trailing off. The old man sees me. Blinks his shark eyes sleepily, not believing it.

"Criminals responsible for atrocity," says the Second, rotely.

I throw off my helmet and break into a trot, weaving between the rows of gleaming statues, gaining speed.

The First shoves the Second on the shoulder, points at me frantically.

"Killers!" booms the Third, clueless, as the Second gives him a push.

I launch myself upward, rising above the wooden wall in a single bound. My body is a majestic suit of golden armor, soaring. I thrust out my rippling metallic arms like wings. At the top of my arc, at my perfect zenith, I gaze down. In my shadow, the Triumvirate gape up at me.

Scared old men with dirty minds and clean hands.

Once, I had a little brother named Chima. He slept with his mouth open. Together, we conquered a wall and built our lives in its safety. Our wall was made to shelter and protect. Others are made to confine and control. But no wall yet built can deflect the knifing flight of blame. The sin circles above, waiting for its moment. And one day it will strike its true target.

My fingers collapse into fists. Legs brace for impact. The three old men hold each other and wail for mercy. But there is no mercy.

At last, I am ready to sin.

BLOOD MEMORY

The hideous child sat up in its cradle and shrieked in delight, "I am old as an oak in the woods, but I never saw a sight such as this!"

—"Fairy Changeling," a folktale
(date unknown)

When Beatrix was diagnosed, I made a promise to her that I would do everything I could to heal her. It's not a promise I ever intended to break.

She's my daughter, no matter what or how hard it is. My MawMaw used to set me on her lap and tell me that our blood is all we're given and it's all we can hope to leave behind. Sure, little Bea was an odd duck. She didn't talk much or cry or laugh like the other children. She just stared—with eyes like stones—looking for patterns in sunlight or in the carpet or wallpaper. The doctors couldn't make heads or tails of her. So, they called it autism and left it at that.

But I promised her.

Now, staring into my twelve-year-old daughter's black, unblinking eyes, I'm telling myself that again and again. Bea clings to me, her body leaning halfway out of the teleporter gate. Her thin fingers claw at my forearm and my ears buzz from the sucking hiss of the machine's open mouth. Her dark brown face is empty, emotionless as always, and the ends of her long black braids are skimming through the oil-gleam of the gate's surface, lost and reappearing in spitting rainbows of color.

"Mama," she says, and I can't tell if she's in pain.

Nothing ever came easy for my little Bea.

This girl may have been born with my same dark eyes, but I could never pretend to understand what she sees from behind those flat mirrors. The doctors put her on the spectrum, but if I'm telling myself the truth—and now is the time, why not?—I always felt like there was somebody else trapped within my daughter's body, something else, watching me from inside her skin.

"Mama," she says, face flashing with light. "It's pretty."

Bea's lips curl into the ghost of a smile and for an instant I catch sight of a different person—a purer reflection of myself and of my husband, too. But I can't let myself think about him right now.

Bea's fingernails are tracing hot ravines down my arm as she pulls me closer. I manage to swallow a moan, molars clamping down on the skin of my cheeks. The familiar words surge through my mind like a prayer.

You are my baby. You are my blood. My baby. My blood.

I've been forcing these words through my mind for a long time, picking them up like rocks and carrying them with me since the day Beatrix and I met each other in a dark hospital room. In the stink of ozone and fear, both of us were so close to crossing over to the other side. Taking her in my arms that day, I saw her little face, those eyes, and I knew in my heart she would never be the person I imagined my daughter might be.

Nothing ever came easy. Not even in our *post-transmission* world.

The teleporter gates give us what we need, when we need it. Drop something into the gate and it's broken down to atoms, sent over as information, and put back together again in another place. The thing is destroyed, and then reborn.

It's only the pattern of it that's important.

If you know the pattern of a thing—even a strange, broken thing—then you can piece it back together. In the end, we're all just patterns, and our babies are the patterns we leave behind, echoes of ourselves that grow louder instead of fading.

Those gates sure changed the world.

Wars gave them to us. Military people fired the first teleporter gates like missiles, scooping up buildings and bunkers where terrorists hid. Then mining companies started pushing industrial versions into solid rock, processing whole mountains. NASA put one on the International Space Station and they started flinging more into space, to the moon and Mars and Europa. Here on Earth, vending machines could suddenly deliver anything. By now, omnigates are an everyday appliance, like a dishwasher or a garbage disposal. Most people have one at home for throwing away trash or receiving deliveries.

Ours is the size of a big trash can with a lid on top. We keep it in the basement.

Turns out, knowing the pattern is enough to put *things* back together, but not people. The trip through a gate breaks anything that lives. What comes out looks the same as what went in, but it's crazy, spitting and screaming and dying within seconds. There's something—some pattern of the mind—that gets lost in there.

At night, with my husband asleep beside me, I've often wondered if the thing that can't find its way out is a person's soul. I think maybe the mortal parts of us get sent over, but not the divine—the weightless part that lives on even after our bodies are gone.

The people in lab coats put one of everything through the gate—a Noah's ark of insanity. After I became a mother, I watched the videos online. Monkeys writhing out with black eyes and bared fangs, choking on their own tongues. Pigs and cats and lab mice crawling out as dried, dying husks. Nematodes, the stupid little worms, they come through fine, wiggling and happy.

Maybe worms don't have souls. Or, who knows, maybe they're just at peace?

On the day Bea was born, I already knew something was wrong before we reached the hospital. The unborn baby didn't feel right, a painful knot inside me. My husband, Kemper, was holding my hand and grinning with excitement. He had a timer that he bought special for this occasion hanging around his neck, like a gym coach.

But I just felt a deep, gut-wrenching sense of dread.

Later, wearing a backless hospital gown under fluorescent lights, I fought to give birth. Hour after hour, I pushed, my arms swollen and marked with purple-blue gashes from the IVs, my vision flashing red from squeezing my eyes closed so tight. Breathing through my teeth, I tried to focus on the next ten seconds.

For thirty hours, I lived ten seconds at a time.

I remember the fat drops of rain that thumped like moths against the black windows of the delivery room. A freak storm was growing in the night, dark waterfalls cascading down from vacuum-kissed heights. As the gale raged, each droplet exploded against cold glass, pulling its neighbors down into the abyss.

Doctors said the baby couldn't get positioned. Worst case, they'd order up a C-section and take her out that way. But I wasn't through trying.

When the lightning storm hit, nobody came right away. The overhead lights blinked out and emergency backups flickered on, glowing crimson like dying embers. Nurses were sprinting through the dim hallway outside, yelling about a fire. Kemper held my hand and we waited until a nurse finally rushed inside.

One look at her face and I knew.

That feeling of wrongness inside me had become something real and hard and utterly impossible to accept. The surgery room was out of commission, the roads out. Necessary equipment was broken. Necessary people were not present. The baby was upside down and she couldn't be born without killing me. In this storm, on this night, there were no safe possibilities and no fairy-tale endings.

Only premature good-byes.

I'm not sure when I noticed the technician standing at the door. Over his paper surgical mask, I could see his eyes were a pale yellow. Greedy, somehow. A rash of pulpy scars traced out from under the mask, veering up toward his ear. He was breathing funny under there, kind of wheezing—maybe from excitement at the emergency, or maybe from whatever deformity lay hidden.

He shuffled into the room, carrying a dark promise. The nurse wouldn't look at him, but she gave the man his space while he went about his business.

Speaking quickly, he said he was a technician for a special machine—a remote gate designed to remove tumors from the human body. Using it to target a baby would be simple, he said. A teleporter gate could be generated around the contours of my unborn child and she could be whisked right out of me. She could be saved.

There were no guarantees, except that Bea would die if we did nothing.

I listened to his promises with my breath coming in sharp pants, sweat pooled in the hollow of my throat. Numb from the waist down, I was nearly delirious after a day of not sleeping and choking down Dixie cups of ice shards.

Nothing ever came easy for my Beatrix. Not from the very start.

Kemper took my hand, already shaking his head *no*. Tears were shining in his eyes. That stupid timer was still hanging around his neck.

But the path had become clear to me.

"I can't lose her. I won't," I said.

"We can't," he told me. "You've seen what happens to—"

Anger crept in, tightening my grip on his hand.

"No," was all I could say.

"You have to accept this," he said. "We have to let go."

"Her name is Beatrix," I said.

He closed his eyes and those tears did fall.

"She wasn't meant to be," he said.

"I can't," I repeated. "I would rather die."

The wind threw itself against the window then, blasting the wall of raindrops into random streaks of light and darkness.

"Honey," Kemper said, opening his eyes and wiping a forearm across his face. "Whatever you decide. I'm with you. But *please*—"

"Yes," I said to the technician. "Do it."

My husband's face went a little empty then. His military bearing crept back into his stance and his spine straightened up. *This is how he survived deployment,* I thought to myself. *Going blank is how you make it through the hard parts.*

Kemper stepped back as the technician wheeled his machine over.

It happened quickly. I signed a paper. Nurses gathered, murmuring. The machine splayed crooked white fingers of plastic around my bulging stomach like a skeletal paw. A strange humming came from inside it, almost like a tune. It must have been the ultrasound targeting, locking on to the baby inside me. For one second, I glimpsed her face on a gray-scale monitor, pixelated and perfect, thumb curled in her mouth. My Beatrix was so close I could almost feel her weight over my chest.

I am your mother, I thought. *I will keep you safe.*

An alert chimed. The machine was ready.

The technician nodded at me, his feline eyes wide over the mask.

Across the room, Kemper was silhouetted against the hallway lights. I could see that his face was in his hands, his shoulders shuddering. I raised an arm, the IV dangling like a puppet string. It will be okay, I tried to say.

The universe will give us this one.

After a flash and a puff of ozone, the world went still. The only truth left was the clear ringing in my ears—a simple song that proved I was still alive. Looking down at myself, I bit back a scream as my stomach deflated grotesquely, the

slack skin falling in on itself like a building with a dyna-
mited foundation. I realized I could feel the horrific alien
fingers of the teleporter reaching *inside*.

Beatrix was gone. The life inside me had been ripped
from the warmth of my womb and sent to some cold, beautiful place.

"Success," whispered the technician.

My Beatrix, tiny and perfect, lay inside a clear acrylic
receiving chamber that had been retrofitted onto the
machine. Squirming like a grub, steam was curling off her
bloody body. She screamed, just once, like she was surprised
at her own existence.

"Is she okay?" I asked.

Nurses swarmed around the receiving tray. Between their
busy elbows and hips I could see only snatches of my now-
silent baby. They cleaned off the blood and amniotic fluid,
throwing away layer after layer of towels, each less bloody
than the last.

"Is she okay?!" I asked again, voice rising.

Three sets of eyes turned to me over surgical masks. The
nurse in the middle was holding Beatrix in her arms, the
baby swaddled tightly in a clean hospital blanket. I saw fear
in the woman's eyes, a quivering across her forehead.

Three steps and then the baby was in my arms, handed
to me quick, like a bomb.

Beatrix's pudgy face was pinched and bruised from her
time trying to be born. She was a dark-skinned little thing,
with a layer of fine black hair covering her body and tiny

tangles of black fuzz sprouting from her head. Her eyes were open wide already, calm and watchful as an old crow.

My daughter was the first and only human being born to teleportation.

Kemper's arms closed around my shoulders as he planted kiss after kiss on my temple and cheek. I simply held Bea and looked down at her. She looked back at me with eyes like a bird had pecked two holes in her face.

"Something's wrong," I said to Kemper. "Look at her eyes."

"Nothing's wrong," he said, hugging us both. "She's got your eyes, honey. She just got them early."

And then Bea seemed to look past me toward the storm-battered window. Turning, I saw only an empty wall of dark glass. Then I noticed how the dim lights from the machine were illuminating silver veins of falling water, forming a kind of pattern.

The infant smiled then, impossibly, her tiny face crinkling like a mask.

Goose bumps erupted down the backs of my arms and a sense of horrible regret settled over my heart. Closing my eyes to the sight of her leering face, I pulled the baby against my chest and squeezed her.

Just a face spasm, I told myself. *Normal. Normal for a sweet baby.*

And then I made myself think the thoughts that I needed to have.

She is my daughter. She is my blood.

When I dared to look at Beatrix again, that devilish smile was gone.

The baby was fine. Every examination showed that. Bea had become proof that maybe, at a certain age, the gates wouldn't wipe a person's mind and force them to go insane. Maybe the brain of an unborn child was too undeveloped to comprehend whatever shapeless things lurked in that millisecond of teleportation.

Bea was fine. But she was never normal.

Over the next six years, Kemper and I watched our black-eyed infant grow into a beautiful little girl. She learned to speak a little, and even to read. She was small, but she had a laser focus that she wielded with singular intent. The things she loved were impossible to keep from her.

We got her a kitten when she was six.

Booker T. Washington was a little pink-nosed ball of orange fur, with claws like pinpricks and the sweet habit of ramming his head into our ankles. We called him Booker T. for short. Kemper and I carried the kitten into Bea's room, both of us smiling and hopeful. But as we watched Bea's flat, expressionless face . . . our hope started to fade.

Bea had other things on her mind.

Sitting on her bedroom floor, she was hunched over, as usual, carefully placing her blocks one by one. The room was littered with toys, a chaos of color spread over every square inch of space. Kemper bent down to release Booker T., and the kitten tumbled and bounded around the clutter for a little while, ignored.

After ten minutes, Kemper left to set up Booker T.'s litter box. He tried to hide it, but I could see the disappointment in his tired shoulders. My mouth opened as he left, but there was nothing I could say to make Bea normal.

I lowered myself to my knees, stroked my little girl's hair.

"Oh, Bea," I whispered, watching her pick up another brightly colored block and replace it in a slightly different position. Looking into her face, I was startled, catching sight of that horrible little smile fading from the corners of her mouth. Eyes downcast, she was staring at the colorful blocks with dark fascination.

I stood up, heart pounding.

Dizzy, I stumbled over the chaos of blocks and toy cars and dolls, climbing straight onto Bea's little bed and looking down. I saw the wooden blocks hadn't been thrown randomly. No, each one was carefully laid in its place. Eyes blurry with sudden tears, I saw that cursed *pattern*.

Bea flung herself onto her back, arms outstretched.

The blocks curled away from her body in a perfect imitation of the shimmering depths of a teleporter gate. Oranges and reds faded to blues and purples, all in weaving lines that sprouted from my daughter in rootlike curls and twists. The pattern of the gate was right there on her floor, frozen in its incredible complexity.

And my Bea lay inside it, her black braids spread out like streaks of oil.

"Sweet Bea?" I asked, not expecting an answer. "What did you make, honey?"

My normally silent six-year-old daughter looked up at me with her lips twisted back into that grin, her black eyes twinkling.

"Inside," she said.

I put her through that teleporter before she was even born. It was my choice to do it because I couldn't lose her. She was so little and helpless.

"No," I whisper.

"Pretty *inside*, Mama."

"Bea," I said, lips gone numb. "No, honey."

The madness in those angles and colors was suddenly too much. Compulsively, I stepped down and began to kick the pattern apart. Bea howled and I kept kicking. I had to destroy it before Kemper could see, before my husband could realize that our Beatrix had been born into a different world. Our baby had sojourned through a nameless land beyond all sanity and she *remembered it.*

By the time Kemper came to the door, I was holding Bea in my arms, rocking and soothing her as she sobbed.

I destroyed the pattern that day, but it always came back.

Bea's coordination was delayed, but as soon as she could hold a crayon, the lines spilled out on reams of butcher paper. Somehow, her chubby little fingers could unleash patterns of light and darkness with the precision of a supercomputer. And as she got older, Beatrix herself began to appear in the images. A little girl's self-portrait, made of black circles, lost in a storm of color.

Sometimes, other shapes emerged in the drawings: outlines of spire-like buildings with stairways at impossible angles; smudges of color that seemed to shimmer like grease; and the primitive beginnings of embryonic, inhuman faces.

Every new drawing I saw felt like swallowing a needle.

Often, I would find Bea lying in her bed with Booker T. asleep at her feet, surrounded by pages and pages of the uncanny drawings, the thick construction paper infected with that horrendous, eye-wrenching pattern. Sometimes blobs of crayon were caked into topographical patterns like the landscape of an alien planet, or I'd find hundreds of ragged holes that seemed to stare like the compound eyes of an insect.

I got religious about throwing them away.

At first, Bea would scream when I balled up her drawings and threw them in the trash. But that stopped when she realized where the paper was going. The omnigate in our basement teleported garbage straight to a massive sorting facility somewhere else, thousands of miles away.

Beatrix began to follow me around the house during the day while Kemper was away working at the army base. At first, I liked having her near me. Then I realized she was waiting for the trash to be emptied. Once we were in the basement, she would stand on the next-to-last step. The plastic guard on the omnigate mostly blocked the light from inside, but at that exact angle on the stairs, Bea's face would flash with the pattern.

Bea lived for that shining moment—the harsh angles

of her face would smooth, eyes drinking the light. Soon enough, I lived for it, too. Seeing her in that moment felt like catching a glimpse of the daughter I might have had.

I was watching drowsy television with Kemper, well after Bea's bedtime, when the high-pitched shrieking launched us both off the couch. At first, I thought it was the squeal of metal from a car crash outside—nothing human, surely.

But then I realized it—and other, worse sounds—were coming from inside.

Kemper ran to the basement door and threw it open. As he thundered down the stairs, I turned and ran for Bea's bedroom. Flipping on the lights, I saw only the pattern in blocks again, spread out around her bed. Bea was gone.

Then I heard Kemper shouting her name.

I found him at the bottom of the dark basement stairs, his back to me, the crackling light of the omnigate casting his shadow across the concrete floor. The flimsy plastic guard lay on the ground, twisted off. And at the mouth of the gate, her body silhouetted by its hot, shifting light, stood my little girl.

In her arms, a wriggling mass of shredded fur was screaming and clawing pathetically. Booker T., insane, orange fur falling off his skin in clumps, was wailing like a human, coughing blood over her forearms.

"Bea! What did you do?!" I shouted.

Kemper lunged forward and snatched the cat away, covering it up so that I couldn't see. Clutching the squirming bundle to his chest, he rushed past me up the stairs. Halfway up, he stopped to look down at me for a split second.

"Oh my God, Bea," he said. "Oh my dear God."

As Kemper took the cat outside, I flew down the stairs to Bea's side.

"Honey? Honey? Are you okay?" I asked.

"Kitty," said Beatrix. "I showed kitty."

"Showed him what, Bea?" I ask, checking her hands and arms. She must have pushed him through the gate and pulled him back. "What did you show the kitty?"

A familiar dark smile played at the corners of her mouth, then faded, like a sea creature sinking into the shadow of the ocean. This close, I could see the spatters of thick blood dotting the skin of her face.

"Inside," she said.

I watched my own hands leap away from her then. I could feel a stranger standing in front of me—an otherness that did not belong here in this world.

She's the wrong one, I thought to myself, closing my eyes. *This thing is not my daughter.*

Telling myself to breathe, I shut down that thinking. I opened my eyes and made myself wrap my arms around Beatrix, pulling her limp body against mine. Watching her bloody, expressionless face, I forced the necessary words into my head. I picked them up like a pile of bricks and I carried them with me.

You are my daughter. You are my blood.

"I want to go inside, Mama," she said to me. "Please."

After that, we locked the basement door. Kemper buried Booker T. in the backyard with nothing to mark the spot. We tried to forget.

I took away Bea's blocks and her coloring books.

Lying in bed with Kemper, staring at a dark ceiling, I couldn't help but whisper my fears out loud.

"Would it be better . . . if she hadn't of, hadn't been . . ."

"Don't say that, baby," whispered Kemper, and I felt his warm hand close over mine. "She'll grow out of this. She's got challenges, but we can do this."

"Yeah, but . . ." I let it stretch out.

"She's our daughter," Kemper said flatly.

To be honest, deep down, I knew Bea would go back someday.

Beatrix is twelve years old on the day that it happens. On my way home from the grocery store, I see the smoke and stomp on the accelerator. Sirens wail in the distance. Our neighbors stand outside their houses, watching with concerned looks as flames lick through our roofline.

I charge through the open front door.

"Kemper?" I call. A haze of smoke clings to the air, but I can't see where the fire is coming from. "Bea?"

I check her room. Empty.

The rest of the small house is empty, too. I see half a graham cracker still sitting on the kitchen table. The door to the basement is slightly open.

Hesitating, I pull it open wider and call into the darkness. "Guys?!"

Nothing.

Catching a faint glimmer of light slithering over the concrete block walls at the bottom of the stairs, I take one step down. And then another.

"Bea?"

The reinforced plastic guard we bought has been torn off the teleporter. An ax from the shed lies beside it, bluish light reflecting off the nicked blade.

A low moan builds deep in my throat.

Reaching the last step, I see my husband's legs. Kemper is lying on his stomach but my mind can't process all of this right away. Legs, all I see are legs.

Legs coming out of the shimmering mouth of the teleporter.

"Kemper!" I shriek. There is an animal raggedness to my voice that I don't recognize. My breath is coming in high-pitched gasps. Falling to my knees, I latch my hands on his ankles and yank him out of the teleporter.

It's like dragging a block of wood.

"What did you do?!" I shout. "Beatrix! *What did you do?!*"

With all my might, I roll Kemper over onto his back. He stares up at me with glassy eyes that have gone white. His brown face has turned the color of ash, withered and slack. His jaw moves once or twice, his tongue swollen and purple.

"A . . . a long time in there." He coughs out the words.

"Honey, honey stay with me," I chant, but his head is already falling back. A choking sound comes from deep in his throat. I lift his head as his chest convulses, trying to clear his airway. Then, seeing his twisted face, I realize that what's left of my husband isn't choking. It's laughing. Trying hard to laugh, anyway. But he can't.

Instead, he dies.

In shock, I kick away from his body, the concrete hard and cold on my tailbone. Something loud crashes in the fire upstairs, and I hug my knees to my chest. No tears are coming. Nothing. I can't feel my face. My arms and legs must belong to somebody else. I notice one of Bea's crumpled drawings on the floor, fallen before it could go into the omnigate. Watching myself move, I pick it up.

I open the drawing slowly, with shaking fingers.

It's a picture of Bea, smiling and happy. She is holding hands with her daddy and mommy. The frenzied, wavy lines of the pattern warp the space around us.

I turn to the teleporter gate. The glowing rectangle winks and dances. I can almost hear words under its static murmur. I can almost see her smile.

Bea is gone. She went home.

My blood.

There are only so many relationships that exist—only so many ways of being human. We start out as children. And, like puzzle pieces rattling in a box, most of us eventually find a connection—we turn into wives and husbands. Before it's all over, many of us find that we've become parents ourselves. And if we're lucky, we get to become grandparents, uncles and aunts, cousins and siblings.

In the end, it's only blood that matters.

MawMaw used to say that the blood of your folks and their folks was "upstream." That's the blood that's come down to you. The "downstream" blood represents the ties we share with our children and their children—it's what we give of ourselves to our babies.

She is my daughter, not a thing.

A mama does anything for her babies. She protects that downstream blood, always, because it matters more than her own. When it's all over and we blink good-bye and let go of our last breath—it's only our blood that we leave behind.

Staring into that infernal spitting pattern and listening to my house burn, pendulous tears finally well into my eyes. My baby is gone, and so is my husband. The gate took everything.

Then Bea's thin brown arm lunges out of the teleporter.

I shriek as her scrawny fingers lock onto my arm like a pair of handcuffs. The disembodied arm disappears into the pattern on the gate's surface. Trying to pull away, I stare into that swirling abyss.

And her dark face materializes.

Those black eyes that we share are wide open and twinkling with happiness. Her lips are curled into a brilliant smile as her head and shoulders emerge. For the first time in her life, she looks like a normal twelve-year-old girl.

"Mama!" she says. "Come and see."

I close my hand over hers and hold on, repeating my mantra, pulling my forearm against her demonic strength.

"Mama," she says, digging her nails into my arm. "It's so pretty inside."

"What have you done, Bea?" I ask.

Bea's eyes flicker down to the corpse of her father, his face aged a thousand years. Her smile falters just a little bit.

"You hurt your daddy," I say, the back of my throat thick with tears.

"It was too bright, Mama," she says.

"Don't call me that."

She frowns now, a dimple appearing between her eyebrows. She is my own sweet baby. I did this to her.

Blinking, my tears come free and streak down my face.

"What are you?" I ask.

Bea leans forward, face brightening. Her breath is hot on my cheek and excitement pulses behind her eyes. Her fingers are so tight on my arm.

"I'm your blood," she says.

The only thing we're given. All we can hope to leave behind.

"We're the same," she says. "Our eyes. Not like Daddy."

No, no.

She is my daughter.

She is my blood, goddamn it.

I blink and this time I feel no tears. I made a promise to my daughter.

I will not lose her. I would rather die.

"Will it . . ." I stop, losing my nerve.

Taking a shuddering breath, I start again.

"Will it hurt?" I ask.

The glow from the gate shimmers and hisses. The hot light from it has never been reflected in her abyssal eyes. Those same eyes I have.

"Oh yes, Mama," she whispers, smiling wide.

FOUL WEATHER

Some things you can't figure out. Not even with a whole heap of scratch paper and a ribbon of data from a chattering teletype machine. Not before time runs out. And time is like progress—she's not stopping for anybody.

The answer is out there, though, in the weather.

Foul weather breeds foul deeds. Something my mother used to say. She said it even when I was a kid, before I ever went into the forecasting business. Before I had a career as a young man and then computers showed up and the whole science of meteorology went and left me behind. Before I became just an old man with his pencils and maps.

Back then, I thought my mother was foolish. Thought she was just making it up off the top of her head when she said things like that. But now I know better. Those sayings come from somewhere. An old, forgotten place where time has worn the words down hard and shiny as coins. When I think back on it, I figure my ma had a lot more wisdom than I ever gave her credit for.

Mothers are like that.

It was a long, long time before I could sit down here at my kitchen table and gather the tools of my old trade. Before I could spread out an obsolete weather map and flatten it down without my hands shaking. Weight the corners. Sharpen my pencils. Try not to think of that damnable day until my maps are clean and smooth, the raw weather data bound and ready, and my theory on what went impossibly wrong finally laid out in crisp clean pencil lines.

Patterns of weather. Patterns of anger.

The memory of Flight 7126 is a lingering wound in my mind. There is a woman's face that has stayed with me for years, like a nasty scar. In the second before she died, her eyes were wide and black. Her lips were cracked with frostbite. When she spoke, I could see she had a mouth full of stained teeth. And even though it was awfully loud on that airplane, her words sliced straight through the bedlam and rang in my ears clear as a bell.

The flight landed safe, understand. The storm was rough—rougher than you can imagine—but all of us made it through. All but her. And the odd thing was, when we touched down, not one of us passengers could seem to recognize the other. Husbands and wives, mothers and children, anonymous folks. The tires bit into the tarmac and we rolled to a stop with so many questions lodged in our throats.

But, like I said, the answer is in the weather, see?

On my map, I can chart it out plain as day. I don't need one of those damned computers to know what I'm looking at. Flight 7126 was headed north over the Arabian Sea. Five hundred miles east of Somalia. That gnarled horn of Africa rooting blindly out into the water. During monsoon season, the Somali jet stream comes howling off those barren plains and spills out over the open sea. And on that day, I believe the wind carried something terrible with it.

I always take the window seat. As former meteorologist and chief weather forecaster for the thirty thousand or so folks in greater Sequoyah County, it's almost a compulsion of mine to sit over the wing and watch the weather patterns unfold. I like to say that riding in an airplane is my version of a biologist's field expedition. I'm at peace up there among the cloud formations and fronts and thermoclines.

You can plot and analyze the behavior of every weather phenomenon happening from the Ozarks to the Tibetan Highlands, but the trick is to get out there and see it evolve—learn where the patterns came from, where they're going and why. Sure, a computer can predict where Jupiter is going to be in a thousand years, to the centimeter, probably, but I defy you to show me the man or computer who can grasp the full complexity of a simple country thunderstorm.

It is an ancient and uncontrollable thing. The weather puts awe into my heart. It has since I was old enough to squint into a sunset.

And this storm . . . let me tell you, she was magnificent. A towering armada of cumulonimbus clouds, plowing over the sea in battle formation. Bruised and throbbing, laced through with lightning strikes like impurities through marble. It was a classic configuration—a flanking line of rolling cumulus clouds followed by the main tower, anvil-shaped, coming at us low and headstrong over shadowed water, dead flat on the bottom but steepled ten thousand feet high. The sea down there must have been hot and angry. Spewing raw energy up into the air, fueling that looming thing above.

One minute the sun was hard and round as a cat's eye shooter marble and the next it blinked out behind the beast. We were all of us thrown into twilight and a dozen conversations trailed off.

I don't know how to describe it, but the mood *darkened*. The engine seemed to drop an octave, taking on a hoarse wail. I could feel the vibration surging through the walls, straining against the floor under my feet. Like a voice was trapped in the corners of things, trying to whisper secrets to me in a dead language.

There was a perfectly nice older lady sitting across the aisle. A gray-hair with chunky reading glasses and one of those wispy scarves around her neck. She was knitting with long needles and I found myself imagining what it would be like to snatch her needles away. To dig my fingers into her graying bun of hair, push a blunt needle up under those reading glasses. Over her cheek and under her sagging eyelid. Hold her head tight as she struggled in my arms.

The lady glanced over at me like she could read my mind. She had no expression on her face, just this dead glazed look in her half-lidded eyes. I turned right away, dumbfounded by my own troubled thoughts, but not before I saw it. Just a flash, but unmistakable—a sudden snarl on her lip, there and gone.

I got it, then. That nice old lady was thinking evil thoughts. Just like me.

And then we were inside the storm.

The armada had risen up from below and consumed our little pocket of air wrapped in metal. A spatter of jet-speed hail hit the plane, pinging into it like ball bearings. It was as if the storm were trying to skin us, trying to pry open every seam and decapitate every bolt to get at the people inside. The hum of the engines dropped again and I'm not sure how to say it but that strange twilight atmosphere took on real *weight*. Like diving too deep, the pressure crushing in on your sinuses from every angle at once.

A few people started to cry, then.

The man behind me began murmuring to himself. Strange talk about green waters and dead branches and gates. Right away, I got this image in my head of how he might look with his throat slit. Head cocked to the side, tongue straining as he tried to gulp pressurized air. Blinking my eyes, I tried to shake the vision out of my brain. But the darkness of the storm had settled in.

I heard him make an odd squeak, and then I made a bad decision.

I twisted around and snuck a look between the seats. In that sliver of space, I found the familiar overweight guy. He was propped back in his seat, uncomfortable, wearing a foot brace and a Panama hat. Blue Hawaiian shirt, white pants. The guy had a silver pen gripped in one pudgy hand. And the tip of the pen, well, he had it jammed under the nail of his index finger, the broken fingernail tilted up and cracked like a ship pushing through an ice sheet.

Blood was throbbing out in scarlet spurts, spattering onto his pants. The fella had a smile on his sweaty face, like a jack-o'-lantern with the candle blown out. Eyes big and empty and dark.

And giggling. That was the squeak I'd heard.

I nearly jumped out of my skin when the flight attendant clamped her fingers onto my shoulder. What with me staring through the seats like a three-year-old kid who won't sit still. I guess I was embarrassed. I put on an automatic polite smile and looked up at her.

My smile faded quick.

It was her eyes, understand. A thin gold chain hung limp across her freckled chest. And her eyes glittered the same as the dull metal—just no life in them. Only the dead mechanical reflection of splintered lightning in the darkness outside. I tried to speak, but my voice caught in my throat and all I could do was carp my mouth.

I think that, somehow, she knew what was about to happen. She saw it.

To this day I remember that flight attendant very well, which is odd because I only caught that one glimpse of her. A skinny lady in a bad-fitting polyester blue uniform. Smoky-black panty hose. Little blue shoes with a gold buckle. Her mouth was open to ask me something. Or maybe to tell me something.

But the plane ripped open before she could speak.

I remember her hair sort of shivered, like a wave of static electricity was washing through. Then the pale white ceiling dimpled in. A giant was knocking hard out there, asking to be let inside and not taking no for an answer. And then the raging sky opened up behind her head.

Most people don't realize how dense our atmosphere really is. Honest to goodness, at sea level people are like fish swimming underwater. Wave your arm and you can feel the nitrogen and oxygen bouncing off. But thirty thousand feet up is a whole different equation. The upper troposphere is a place where the atmosphere is a quarter as dense as on the surface. You can't find two molecules of oxygen to rub together to save your life. Thin air, they say.

It's the domain of storms, and not of men.

When the roof opened up, the plane itself groaned like a bull elephant after being shot in the lungs. Most of the passengers started to scream then, but not all of them. Some started to laugh, God help us.

For my part, I was silent, still staring into the face of the flight attendant as the cabin depressurized. That furious African storm had rushed across the sea to greet us and had finally made her way inside the airplane.

We were all together at last.

The flight attendant was yanked up into the air like a puppet on steel gauge wires. That hole in the ceiling gaped behind her, a hungry mouth. Somehow her arms and legs darted out with uncanny strength and she caught herself. Newspapers and magazines and trash whipped past her and out into the raging abyss.

Her eyes never left mine, even while they were filling with blood.

In that instant, the flight attendant spoke to me. Her face was nearly out of the plane and frost had already scabbed on her nose and cheeks. She perched above me with the tendons leaping out of her neck, arms splayed out like a spider, her bleeding fingers gripped onto jagged metal. Her lips were moving through a strained smile, and I don't know how, but her words found my ears.

"Black planets roll" is what she said to me.

It was then I saw her mouth was full of stained teeth. And though it was a vague feeling, I got the idea there were more rows of teeth in her mouth than there ought to be. She blinked once; her retinas had hemorrhaged and I thought of an extinct shark. She smiled down at me like the specter of death and I wondered at the strength she had to keep from being torn from the airplane. I marveled at how her strange urgent words had somehow cut through the cyclone and augured into the middle of my head.

And since I'm being honest here, I'll tell you something else: I was *glad* when the flight attendant lost her grip and rude ugly physics folded her thin body in half and she disappeared through that ragged hole. *Glad.*

Because when she flew away, I felt the darkness go with her—flapping on bat's wings out into the heart of the storm. A human sacrifice.

Here in my little house in eastern Oklahoma, I keep the windows open. I've always enjoyed letting the weather inside. I like to spread out the welcome mat, so to speak, let her come on in to say hello and visit awhile. The weather is all around me as I sit in my kitchen, plotting these fronts and pressure zones on an antique weather map. Even now, I can smell the rain-kissed scent of the wind as it sweeps in off the Great Plains. My curtains twist in the breeze and I imagine they're waving hello and good-bye.

I have always loved the weather. Meteorology changed when the computers came and the field marched on ahead and left me behind. But the weather herself always stayed with me. You take the data and plot it and replot it yourself, see? Pressure rises and falls. Fronts advance and retreat. And as the years go by, the patterns seep into your mind. You get a feel for how certain features evolve with time, where the weather came from. Where it's going next, and why.

Here in my kitchen, I get to thinking about that storm sometimes.

The thing that enveloped our plane that day carried a kind of poison with it, I think. That's why I tracked her to where she formed. Along the spine of Somalia, where a wall of hot, humid wind collided with a cold front falling hard and fast. With reams of historical data and pencil shavings and crumbling erasers I followed that monstrous storm all the way back to where she was created. And that's where I found my answer.

In the weather.

Technically, it's in the history book open on my table. Genocide, you understand. My storm rose from a low plateau on the Horn of Africa. They say the fields there were clotted with the blood of butchered tribes. Women and children hacked to pieces. Over four thousand people tore each other apart in a frenzy on the day my storm was born. A nightmare of rape and slaughter that went on until there was nobody left to tell about it. Not a drop more suffering left.

Did the storm cause it? Or did it cause the storm?

Hell, I don't know. It'll take a better forecaster than me to answer that question. Maybe some kid will sit down at a fancy computer and figure it out one of these days.

Foul weather breeds foul deeds.

My mother said it for years, and I ignored her. But she

was right all along. We're each of us a part of the breeze and the rain and the sunlight. The weather is with us always, lurking quiet in the background of our lives. She's a punishing rainstorm while you change a flat tire. The breath of sweet wind on your neck as you kiss a girl out behind the gymnasium. And she is other, darker things.

THE NOSTALGIST

He was an old man who lived in a modest gonfab, and over the last eighty hours his Eyes™ and Ears™ had begun to fail. In the first forty hours, he had ignored the increasingly strident sounds of the city of Vanille and focused on teaching the boy who lived with him. But after another forty hours the old man could no longer stand the Doppler-affected murmur of travelers on the slidewalks outside, and the sight of the boy's familiar deformities became overwhelming. It made the boy sad to see the old man's stifled revulsion, so he busied himself by sliding the hanging plastic sheets of the inflatable dwelling into layers that dampened the street noise. The semitransparent veils were stiff with grime and they hung still and useless like furled, ruined sails.

The old man was gnarled and bent, and his tendons were like taut cords beneath the skin of his arms. He wore a soiled white undershirt and his sagging chest bristled with gray hairs. A smooth patch of pink skin occupied a hollow under his left collarbone, marking the place where a rifle slug had passed cleanly through many decades before. He had been a father, an engineer, and a war-fighter, but for many years now he had lived peacefully with the boy.

Everything about the old man was natural and wrinkled except for his Eyes™ and Ears™, thick glasses resting on the creased bridge of his nose, and two flesh-colored buds nestled in his ears. They were battered technological artifacts that captured sights and sounds and sanitized every visual and auditory experience. The old man sometimes wondered whether he could bear to live without these artifacts. He did not think so.

"Grandpa," the boy said as he arranged the yellowed plastic curtains. "Today I will visit Vanille City and buy you new Eyes™ and Ears™."

The old man had raised the boy and healed him when he was sick and the boy loved him.

"No, no," replied the old man. "The people there are cruel. I can go myself."

"Then I will visit the metro fab and bring you some lunch."

"Very well," said the old man, and he pulled on his woolen coat.

A faded photo of the boy, blond and smiling and happy, hung next to the door of the gonfab. They passed by the photo, pushed the door flaps aside, and walked together into the brilliant dome light. A refreshing breeze ruffled the boy's hair. He faced into it as he headed for the slidewalk at the end of the path. A scrolling gallery of pedestrians passed steadily by. Sometimes the fleeting pedestrians made odd faces at the boy, but he was not angry. Other pedestrians, the older ones, looked at him and were afraid or sad, but tried not to show it. Instead, they stepped politely onto faster slidestrips farther away from the stained gonfab.

"I will meet you back here in one hour," said the old man.

"See you," replied the boy, and the old man winced. His failing Ears™ had let through some of the grating quality of the boy's true voice, and it unsettled him. But his Ears™ crackled back online and, as the slidestrips pulled them away in separate directions, he chose only to wave good-bye.

The boy did not wear Eyes™ or Ears™. Near the time of his birth, the boy had undergone direct sensory augmentation. The old man had seen to it himself. When the boy squinted in just the right way, he could see the velocity trajectories of objects hovering in the air. When he closed his eyes entirely, he could watch the maximum probability version of the world continue to unfold around him. He was thankful for his gift and did not complain about his lessons or cry out when the old man made adjustments or improvements to the devices.

The city is unsafe and I must protect the old man, thought the boy. *He will probably visit the taudi quarter for used gear. Mark his trajectory well,* he told himself. *Remember to be alert to the present and to the future.*

The boy expertly skipped across decelerating slidestrips until his direction changed. Other passengers shied away in disgust, but again the boy did not mind. He walked directly to the center strip and was accelerated to top speed. A vanilla-smelling breeze pushed thin blond hair from his disfigured, smiling face.

The old man smiled as he cruised along the slidewalk. The systematic flow of identical people was beautiful. The men wore dark blue suits and red ties. Some of them carried briefcases or wore hats. The women wore dark blue skirts and white blouses with red neckerchiefs. The men and women walked in lockstep and were either silent or extremely polite. There was a glow of friendly recognition between the pedestrians, and it made the old man feel very glad, and also very cautious.

I must hurry to the taudi quarter and be careful, he thought. *The rigs there have all been stolen or taken from the dead, but I have no choice.*

The old man made his way to the decelerator strip, but a dark-suited businessman blocked his path. He gingerly tapped the man on his padded shoulder. The businessman in the neatly pressed suit spun around and grabbed the old man by his coat.

"Don't touch me," he spat.

For a split second the clean-cut businessman transformed into a gaunt and dirty vagrant. A writhing tattoo snaked down half of his stubbled face and curled around his neck. The old man blinked hard, and the dark-suited man reappeared, smiling. The old man hastily tore himself from the man's grasp and pushed to the exit and the taudi quarter beyond.

Bright yellow dome light glistened from towering, monolithic buildings in the taudi quarter. It reflected off polished sidewalks in front of stalls and gonfabs that were filled with neatly arranged goods laid out on plastic blankets. The old man tapped his malfunctioning Ears™ and listened to the shouts of people trading goods in dozens of languages. He caught the trickling sound of flowing refuse and the harsh sucking sound of neatly dressed people walking through filth. He looked at his shoes and they were clean. The smell of the street was almost unbearable.

The old man approached a squat wooden stall and waited. A large man wearing a flamboyant, filthy pink shirt soon appeared. The man shook his great head and wiped his calloused hands on a soiled rag. "What can I do for you, Drew?" he said.

"LaMarco," said the old man, "I need a used Immersion System. Late model with audiovisual. No olfactory." He tapped his Eyes™. "Mine are beyond repair, even for me."

LaMarco ran a hand through his hair. "You're not still living with that . . . thing, are you?"

Receiving no reply, LaMarco rummaged below the flimsy wooden counter. He dropped a bundle of eyeglasses and earbuds onto the table. One lens was smeared with dried blood.

"These came from a guy got zipped by the militia last week," said LaMarco. "Almost perfect condition, but the ID isn't wiped. You'll have to take care of that."

The old man placed a plastic card on the table. LaMarco swiped the card, crossed his arms, and stood, waiting.

After a pause, the old man resignedly removed his glasses and earbuds and handed them to LaMarco. He shuddered at the sudden sights and sounds of a thriving slum.

"For parts," he coaxed.

LaMarco took the equipment and turned it over delicately with his large fingers. He nodded, and the transaction was complete. The old man picked up his new Immersion System and wiped the lenses with his coat. He slid the glasses onto his face and inserted the flesh-colored buds into his ears. Cleanliness and order returned to the slums.

"Look," said LaMarco, "I didn't mean anything by—"

He was interrupted by the violent roar of airship turbines. Immediately, the old man heard the smack-smack of nearby stalls being broken down. Gonfabs began to deflate, sending a stale breeze into the air. Shouts echoed from windowless buildings. The old man turned to the street. Merchants and customers clutched briefcases and ran hard, their chiseled faces contorted with strange, fierce smiles.

"Go," hissed LaMarco.

The whine of turbines grew stronger. Dust devils swirled across the promenade. LaMarco flipped the wooden countertop over and picked up the equipment-filled crate, cradling it in his powerful arms.

"Another raid," he huffed, and lumbered off through a dark gap between two buildings.

The old man felt wary but calm. When a massive, dead-black sheet of cloth unfurled impossibly from the sky, he was not surprised. He turned and another sheet dropped. A swirling black confusion of sackcloth walls surrounded him. He looked straight up and saw that the convulsing walls stretched for miles up into the atmosphere. A small oval of dome light floated high above. The old man heard faint laughter.

The militia are here with their ImmerSyst censors, he observed.

Two black-clad militiamen strode through the twisting fabric like ghosts. Both wore lightly actuated lower-extremity exoskeletons, the word LEEX stenciled down the side of each leg. Seeing the old man standing alone, they advanced and spread out, predatorily.

A familiar insignia on the nearest officer's chest stood out: a lightning bolt striking a link of chain. This man was a veteran light-mechanized infantryman of the Auton Conflicts. Six symmetric scars stood out on the veteran's cheeks and forehead like fleshy spot welds.

A stumper attached its thorax to this man's face some time ago, thought the old man. *The machine must have been lanced before its abdomen could detonate.*

"This your shack?" asked the scarred veteran.

He walked toward the old man, his stiff black boots crunching through a thick crust of mud mixed with Styrofoam, paper, and shards of plastic and glass.

"No."

"Where'd you get that ImmerSyst?" asked the other officer.

The old man said nothing. The veteran and the young officer looked at each other and smiled.

"Give it here," said the veteran.

"Please," said the old man, "I can't." He clawed the Immersion System from his face. The flowing black censor walls disappeared instantly. He blinked apprehensively at the scarred veteran, shoved the devices deep into his coat pockets, and ran toward the alley.

The veteran groaned theatrically and pulled a stubby impact baton from his belt.

"Fine," he said. "Let's make this easy." He flicked his wrist and the dull black instrument clacked out to its full length. At a trot, he came up behind the old man and swung the baton low, so that it connected with the back of his knees. The impact baton convulsed and delivered a searing electric shock that buckled the old man's legs. He collapsed onto his stomach and was still.

Then he began to crawl with his elbows.

Have to make it out of this alive, he thought. *For the boy.*

The veteran pinned the old man with a heavy boot between the shoulder blades. He lifted his baton again.

A sharp, alien sound rang out—low and metallic and with the tinny ring of mechanical gears meshing. It was not a human voice.

"Stop!" it said, although the word was barely recognizable.

The boy strode into the clearing. The old man, without his Eyes™ or Ears™, noticed that the boy's legs were not quite the same length. He abruptly remembered cobbling them together from carbon fiber scavenged from a downed military UAV. Each movement of the boy's limbs generated a wheezing sigh of pneumatically driven gases. The boy reeked of a familiar oil and hot battery smell that the old man had not noticed in years.

The veteran locked eyes with the small boy and his armored body began to quake. He unconsciously fingered the scars on his face with one hand as he lifted his boot from the old man's back.

The old man rolled over and grunted, "Run, boy!"

But the boy did not run.

"What's this?" asked the younger officer, unfazed. "Your Dutch wife?" The officer popped his impact baton to full length and stood towering over the boy. He leaned down and looked directly into the boy's eye cameras.

"Hey there, toaster oven," said the officer quietly. "Think you're human?"

These words confused the boy, who said nothing.

"Watch out!" came a strangled cry from the veteran. He stood with his knees bent and his left palm extended defensively. His other elbow jutted out awkwardly as he fumbled for his gun. "That is unspecked hardware!" he shouted hoarsely. "Could be anything. Could be military grade. Back away from it!"

The younger officer looked at the veteran uncertainly.

The boy took a hesitant step forward. "What did you say to me?" he asked. His voice was the low, tortured croak of a rusty gate. He reached for the officer with a trembling, three-fingered hand. "Hey," he said.

The officer turned and instinctively swung his impact baton. It thumped against the boy's chest and discharged like a crack of lightning. The blow charred the boy's T-shirt and tore a chunk out of his polyurethane chest-piece, revealing a metal rib cage frame riddled with slots for hardware and housing a large, warm, rectangular battery. The boy sat heavily on the ground, puzzled.

Looking around in a daze, he saw that the old man was horrified. The boy mustered a servo-driven smile that pulled open a yawning hole in his cheek. The old man took a shuddering breath and buried his face in the crook of his elbow.

And the boy suddenly understood.

He looked down at his mangled body. A single vertiginous bit of information lurched through his consciousness and upended all knowledge and memory: *Not a boy*. He remembered the frightened looks of the slidewalk pedestrians. He remembered long hours spent playing cards with the old man. And finally he came to remember the photograph of the blond boy that hung on a plastic hook near the door of the gonfab. At this memory, the boy felt deeply ashamed.

No, no, no, no. I cannot think of these things, he told himself. *I must be calm and brave now.*

The boy rose unsteadily to his feet and adopted a frozen stance. Standing perfectly still removed uncertainty. It made mentals in physical space simpler, more accurate, and much, much faster. The old man had taught the boy how to do this, and they had practiced it together many times.

Ignoring the commands of his veteran partner, the young officer swung his impact baton again. The sparking cudgel followed a simple, visible trajectory. The boy watched a blue rotational vector emerge from the man's actuated hip, and neatly stepped around his stationary leg. The officer realized what had happened, but it was too late: the boy already stood behind him. *The man's hair smells like cigarettes,* thought the boy; and then he shoved hard at a precise spot between the officer's shoulder blades.

The officer pitched forward lightly, but the Leex resisted and jerked reflexively backward to maintain its balance. The force of this recoil snapped the officer's spine somewhere in his lower back. Sickeningly, the actuated legs walked away, dragging the unconscious top half of the officer behind them, his limp hands scraping furrows in the dirt.

The boy heard a whimpering noise and saw the veteran standing with his gun drawn. A line visible only to the boy extended from the veteran's right eye, along the barrel of the pistol, and to a spot on the boy's chest over his pneumatic heart.

Carefully, the boy rotated sideways to minimize the surface area of his body available to the veteran's weapon. *Calm and brave.*

A pull trajectory on the veteran's trigger finger announced an incoming bullet. Motors squealed and the boy's body jerked violently a small distance in space. The bullet passed by harmlessly, following its predicted trajectory. An echoing blast resounded from the blank-walled buildings. The veteran stood for a moment, clutched his sweating face with his free hand, turned, and fled.

"Grandpa!" said the boy, and rushed over to help.

But the old man would not look at him or take his hand; his face was filled with disgust and fear and desperation. Blindly, the old man shoved the boy away and began scrabbling in his pockets, trying frantically to put his new Eyes™ and Ears™ back on. The boy tried to speak, but he stopped when he heard his own coarse noise. Uncertain, he reached out, as if to touch the old man on the shoulder, but did not. After a few long seconds, the boy turned and hobbled away, alone.

The old man grasped the cool, black handrail of the slidewalk with his right hand. He curled his left hand under his chin, pulling his woolen coat tight. Finally, he limped to the decelerator strip and stepped off. He had to pause and breathe slowly three times before he reached the house.

Inside the dim gonfab, he hung his coat on a transparent plastic hook. He wet his rough hands from a suspended water bag and placed cool palms over his weathered face.

Without opening his Eyes™, he said, "You may come out."

Metal rings supporting a curtained partition screeched apart and the boy emerged into a shaft of yellow dome light. The ragged wound in his cosmetic chest carapace gaped obscenely. His dilated mechanical irises audibly spiraled down to the size of two pinpricks, and the muted light illuminated a few blond hairs clinging anemone-like to his scalded plastic scalp. He was clutching the photograph of the blond boy and crying and had been for some time, but there was no sign of this on his crudely sculpted face.

The old man saw the photograph.

"I am sorry," he said, and embraced the boy. He felt an electrical actuator poking rudely through the child's T-shirt, like a compound fracture.

"Please," he whispered. "I will make things the way they were before."

But the boy shook his head. He looked up into the old man's watery blue Eyes™. The room was silent except for the whirring of a fan. Then, very deliberately, the boy slid the glasses from the old man's face, leaving the Ears™.

The old man looked at the small, damaged machine with tired eyes full of love and sadness. When the thing spoke, the shocking hole opened in its cheek again and the old man heard the clear, piping voice of a long-dead little boy.

"I love you, Grandpa," it said.

And these words were as true as sunlight.

With deft fingers, the boy-thing reached up and pressed a button at the base of its own knobbed metal spine. There was a winding-down noise as all the day's realization and shame and understanding faded away into nothingness.

The boy blinked slowly and his hands settled down to his sides. He could not remember arriving, and he looked around in wonder. The gonfab was silent. The boy saw that he was holding a photograph of himself. And then the boy noticed the old man.

"Grandpa?" asked the boy, very concerned. "Have you been crying?"

The old man did not answer. Instead, he closed his eyes and turned away.

PARASITE

A ROBOPOCALYPSE STORY

I dreamed I was breathing.

—Lark Iron Cloud

New War: Final Minutes

When I was a boy, Lonnie Wayne Blanton led me into the deep dark woods and left me there. After I fought my way back out he told me I was a man and I could feel that he was right. Six months later, I led the soldiers of Gray Horse Army right back into the deep dark woods to face the machines of the New War. We fought our way out, but honest to God, I could not tell you what we have become.

—Lark Iron Cloud, MIL#GHA530

Carl is on his ass. Whimpering and clawing and kicking his way backward through the snow. My soldier won't look at me and he won't take my hand and I can't for the life of me understand why until I notice his eyes.

Not where he's looking. But where he *won't* look.

Something black, crawling low and fast on too many legs. And another one. Coming up from under the snow.

Too late.

I don't feel the pincers at first. Just this strong pressure on the base of my neck. I'm in a hydraulic-powered bear hug. I spin around in the slushy snow but there's nobody behind me.

Whatever-it-is has climbed up my back and got a good hold. My knees sag with the lurching weight of it. Crooked black feelers reach around my chest and my spine is suddenly on fire as the thing decides to dig in, a bundle of squirming razor blades.

Shit shit shit—what is this that it hurts so *goddamn much.*

Carl's got his frost-plated rifle up, training it on me. The gun strap hangs stiff and crusty in the arctic breeze. Around us, the rest of my soldiers are screaming and dancing in tight, panicked circles. Some are running. But me and the engineer are having our own little moment here.

"Carl," I wheeze. "No."

My voice sounds hollow from the pain of whatever has got between my shoulder blades. Judging from Carl's blank face I figure I'm not in a very happy spot here. No, sir. That is a full-on nega-*tory.*

Carl lets go of his rifle but the strap catches on his forearm. He stumbles away, gun dangling. Wipes his eyes with shaking fingers, tendons streaking the backs of his hands. His complicated engineering helmet falls off and thunks into the snow, an empty bowl.

He's crying. I could give a shit.

I'm being flayed alive, straining and groaning against black spider legs gripping my body, doing drunken pirouettes in the slush. Knotty black arms slice into the meat of my thighs, sprouting smaller feelers like vines. Others grip my biceps, elbows, forearms, and, goddamn it, even my fingers.

I am in command but I am most definitely not in control. Some of my soldiers are still thrashing. Some aren't. The wounded are crawling and hobbling away as fast as they can, coiled black shapes slicing toward them like scorpions.

Carl's gone now: hightailed it. Left his ostrich-legged tall-walker behind, collapsed awkwardly on its side. Left all of us unlucky dancers behind.

My legs are wrapped too tight now to struggle. A motor grinds as I push against it, reaching back with my arm. I feel a freezing fist-sized plate of metal, hunkered in the warm spot at the base of my neck. Not good.

The machine snaps my arm back into place.

Can't say I'm real sure of what happens next. I got a lot of experience breaking down Rob hardware for Gray Horse Army, though. After a while, you get a feel for how the machines think. How they use and reuse all those bits and pieces.

So, I imagine my guess is pretty accurate.

As I watch the vapor of my last breath evaporate, the parasite on my back jerks and severs my spinal column with a flat, sharpened piece of metal mounted to its head region. My arms and legs go numb, so much dead meat. But I don't fall because the machine's arms and legs are there to hold me up.

And I don't die.

Some kind of cap must fit over the nub of my spine, interfacing with the bundle of nerves there. This is a mobile surgery station leeched onto my neck. Humming and throbbing and exploring, it's clipping veins and nerves and whatever else. Keeping oxygen in my blood, circulating it.

I'm spitting cherry syrup into the snow.

Lonnie Wayne Blanton, my commander, says that this late in the war you can't let anything the enemy does surprise you. He says Big Rob cooks up a brand-new nightmare every day and he's one hell of a chef. Yet here I am. Surprised, again.

The machine is really digging in now. As it works, my eyes and ears start blurring and ringing and singing. I wonder if the scorpion can see what I see. Hear what I hear.

I'm hallucinating in the snow.

A god-sized orange tendril of smoke roils across the pale sky. It's real pretty. Smaller streams fall from it, pouring down like water from drain spouts. Some of the streams disappear behind the trees, others are even farther away. But one of them twists down and drops straight at me. Into my head.

A line of communication.

Big Rob has got me. The thinking machine that calls itself Archos is driving the pulsing thing on my back. A few dozen clicks from here, the architect of the New War is crouched where that fat orange column of transmission ends. Pulling all the strings.

I watch as my dead arms unsling my rifle. Tendons in my neck creak as the machine twists my head, sweeps my vision across the clearing. I'm alone now, and I think I'm hunting.

In the growing twilight, I spot dozens of other orange umbilical cords just like mine. They fall out of the sky into the dark woods around me. As I lurch forward out of the clearing the other lines drift alongside me, keeping pace.

All of us are being dragged in the same direction.

We're a ragged front line of dark shapes, hundreds strong, shambling through the woods toward the scattered remnants of Gray Horse Army. My consciousness begins to fade in and out as my cooling body slogs its way between the trees. The last thing I remember thinking is that I hope Lonnie Wayne don't see me like this. And if he does, well, I hope he puts me down quick.

I don't hear the gunshot itself, just a dry echo in the trees. It's something, though. Enough to wake me up.

I dreamed I was breathing.

The impossible smoke in the sky is gone. All those evil

thoughts disappeared. And the place where Archos lived is empty now. Big Rob must be dead. It's the only explanation.

The New War is over and we won and I'm still here. Still alive, somehow.

I focus on it and the wires of my parasite start to work my legs. Carry me in the direction of the gunshot. Over the charred earth of a weeks-old battlefield. I pass by a titanic spider tank leaning still and cold and heavy against a snowbank. Its armor is pocked with sooty craters, intention light shattered, joints cracked open like lobster claws. And bodies.

Frozen bodies melded with the snow. Stiff uniforms and frostbitten metal. The occasional alabaster patch of exposed frozen flesh. I recognize most of the corpses as Gray Horse Army, but pieces of some other army are here, too. Bodies of the ones who came and fought before we ever knew Archos existed.

Among the trees at the edge of the clearing, I see the others.

A cluster of a dozen or so walking corpses stand huddled, shoulder to shoulder. Silent. Some are still in full uniform, normal-looking save for the clinging clockwork parasites. Others are worse off: A woman is missing her leg, yet she stands steadily on the narrow black appendage of the parasite. One man is shirtless in the cold, skin wind-blasted to a marbled corpse-sheen. All of them are riddled with puckered bullet holes. Cratered exit wounds flapping with icy skin and torn armor.

And I see another, freshly killed.

A still form lies in the snow. Its head is missing, pieces scattered. A parasite lies on its back nearby, coated in rusty blood, slowly flexing its mouth-pieces like a squashed bug.

So that gunshot served a purpose.

These survivors have one combat shotgun left between them. A big man, stooped over with his own size, has got the gun now. Most of his face is hidden in an overgrown beard but I can see his mouth is round and open, a rotten hole. He's moving slow because frostbite has taken all his fingers, but I figure out pretty quick where he's going with that barrel.

They're taking turns killing themselves.

"No," I try to shout, but it comes out a shapeless sob. "No, this is *wrong*."

I shuffle faster, weaving between shredded bodies trapped in permafrost like it was quick-set concrete. None of the survivors pays me much attention. They keep their faces aimed away from the big man, but stand close to grab the shotgun when it falls.

The bearded man has his eyes closed. So he doesn't understand what's happening when I shove the butt of the gun. His blackened nub of a thumb nudges the trigger and the gun thunders and leaps out of his hands. Pieces of bark and a puff of snow drift down from the trees overhead. The slug missed.

Those great black eyes open, mottled with frost, and understanding sets in. With an angry moan, the big man swings at me. His frozen forearm lands like an aluminum baseball bat, propelled by black robotic musculature. It chips off a piece of my elbow, knocks me off balance. Only now do I realize that I'm missing half of my torso. My guts are gone and so is my center of balance. Guess I'm not the steadiest corpse alive.

I drop hard into the snow.

The guy lifts his leg, his long tendons snapping like frozen tree branches, and drops a boot into my stomach cavity. Rib fragments scatter in the snow among shreds of my clothing and flesh. The beard keeps stomping and moaning, destroying my already ruined body in a slow-motion rage.

And I can't feel a goddamn thing.

Then another shot is fired. The booming echo skitters through the trees in unfamiliar lurches. An unidentified weapon.

The next stomping blow doesn't land.

I shove myself into sitting position as something comes out from behind a cracked tree trunk. It is short and gray-skinned, limping. The parasite on its back is blocky, not as graceful as the smoothly ridged humps the rest of us wear. And it's got on a strange uniform, long frozen to warped bone. This thing was a soldier, once.

Not one of ours. A Chinese soldier.

A familiar tendril of orange smoke rises from the new soldier's parasite. It's some kind of bad dream, something the parasite makes me see, yet it feels more real than the ice world around me. The tendril floats like a spiderweb on the wind. Closer and closer.

When it lands on my head, I hear a woman's voice.

"I am Chen Feng. Wandering lost in Dìyù, yet honor-bound to live. I greet you in solidarity, survivor," she says.

The soldier thing is a female. Exposed cheekbones dapple her shrunken face, polished by the weather. She has the grinning toothy mouth of a corpse, yet her words expand into my head like warm medicine.

"Hello?" I ask, watching a flicker of radio communication intertwine with her light. Whoa. She's gone and taught me to speak. *"Where did you come from?"*

"I am the might of Manchuria. A spirit. No longer alive and not yet dead."

"Where are your people?"

"They are as dust. The Northeast Provinces foolishly marched alone. We sought glory and instead were devoured by the jīqì rén. Those consumed rose again into Dìyù. Forced to slaughter our brothers and sisters. The Siberian Russians arrived with vodka and boasts and we slew the Èluósī, too. You dark-skinned ones came on walking tanks, and we rose wearily once more."

"You were waiting for us."

"Your metal soldiers were too fast. The pànduàn cut through our frozen flesh. Raced into the west. And when the final pànduàn defied the great enemy, we heard its screams of rage. The foul deep light was extinguished, and I awoke from Dìyù into another nightmare."

Years. This soldier must have been out here in the cold for *years*. The enormity of her suffering fills my mind.

"We've got to leave here," I say.

Chen Feng doesn't respond. Neither do the others. A hopeless silence settles onto my shoulders like gravity. There is nowhere to go and we all know it. I turn to the horizon, avoiding their faces. And only now do I realize that I can see a kind of leftover orange haze beyond the trees.

It's the place where Archos must have made its final stand. And where I might still find Lonnie Wayne. The man saved my life and brought me into Gray Horse Army. I'm scared to let him see me like this but I've got hurt soldiers who need me.

"We reunite with Gray Horse Army," I say, and begin to limp away.

Our group walks for three days and nights. We don't tire and we don't change pace. The orange mist on the horizon always grows. Our sluggish steps never stop.

I don't notice when Chen Feng stops moving. I'm watching her back and thinking that you could almost mistake her for a human being. Somebody who has been tore up, sure, but a living person. Daydreaming, I walk right past her.

I'm almost killed before I can stop.

The slender silver machine named Nine Oh Two is standing motionless in the snow. A seven-foot-tall humanoid robot with a scavenged rifle on the high ready. Its three eyes are on me, lenses dilating as it absorbs the fact of my existence. It hasn't shot me yet, so it must be trying to classify what it sees.

Am I a severely wounded human being? A broken war machine? Am I dead or alive or what the hell? Nine Oh Two doesn't seem to know and neither do I.

Over the machine's shoulder, I see a little tent shivering in the wind. The structure is wrapped up tight and the interior is throbbing with that rotten orange glow. Some shard of Archos is inside, talking.

I take a step forward.

Nine Oh Two bristles. Thin sheets of ice crack and fall from his joints as the barrel of his gun settles between my eyes.

Familiar smoke rises from the machine's forehead. A line of communication that settles over me. Nine Oh Two points at the snow a few yards away.

"Path blocked, acknowledge. Alternate route indicated. I wish you luck . . . creatures," it says.

All kinds of tracks are in the muddy ice. Regular old footprints, the neatly spaced mineshafts of high-stepping tall-walkers, and the flat-topped mesas left by spider tanks dragging their equipment-filled belly nets over high snowdrifts.

Gray Horse Army passed this way.

———

There are no mirrors out here in the wilderness and I thank the Creator for that.

Without a mirror, it's up to my imagination to guess what Gray Horse Army sees when they look out at us. A shambling group of a dozen corpses following in their tracks, brain-dead and deaf and dumb. Luckily, my imagination isn't that good anymore.

The humans don't travel at night, which is why we catch up to them.

At dusk on the third day, we watch the spider tanks amble into covered-wagon formation. The legged metal giants squat into bunker configurations for the night, encircling the human camp. In the protected clearing, campfires glitter into existence. Soon, rifle scopes wink at us from the tops of the tanks.

Got to keep the zombies at bay.

But we stay at a safe distance. Sway together numbly through the night, the wind cutting moaning tunnels between us. Gray Horse Army does not fire. The war is over, after all. I imagine we're just another one of the odd atrocities left behind in this new world. Not enemies, not yet.

At dawn, there is movement.

A tall-walker pulls up short and the rider watches for maybe half an hour. The rest of the camp is packing up. Groaning tanks stand up, loaded with soldiers. A flock of tall-walker scouts sprint ahead. But before the army moves, two tanks part and a handful of men approach. As they get near, I recognize Lonnie Wayne.

He's shading his eyes and shaking his head in disbelief.

Lonnie shrugs off his battle rifle and tosses it to the man next to him. Unfastens the loop on his sidearm holster, lets the pistol hang low on his hip. Extra ammunition and a knife and a hand radio hang from his belt, flopping as he strides toward us, alone.

"Lark," he calls, voice breaking.

His boots crunch through the brittle morning snow.

I don't react because I can't. My every move is monstrous. To speak is to groan. To move my corpse's puppet arms is to make a mockery of the dead. I'm so ashamed of my injuries. All I can do is stand here, a monster swaying with the wind as the breaking sun turns the ice to light.

Lonnie ignores the others. Gets near enough to look into my face.

"Oh, Lark," he says. "Look what they did to you."

I send all my concentration into the foreign black metal in my head. Push out a glowing wisp of contact that only I can see. Let it settle over Lonnie's hand radio like ghostly fingertips. It doesn't catch, though. He's got man-made equipment and it doesn't work like Rob-built hardware. My light slips right through.

The old man studies me, looks for some reaction. But I can give him nothing.

"I can't leave you like this," he says.

Lonnie draws his pistol, reluctant, eyes shining. Lifts it glinting into the air and extends his arm. My head wobbles as the barrel noses into my temple. This close to death and

I can't scream for Lonnie to stop. All I can think of is how much I miss the feeling of my goddamn heart beating in my chest.

"Lark," he says. "I'm proud of you, kid. You did real good."

The old man pulls back the hammer with his thumb. Drops his index finger into the trigger guard. Wraps it around the cold familiar steel.

"You were a son to me," he says, and he squeezes his mouth into a hard line. Looks away, keeping his blue eyes wide to stop the tears from falling out.

Then his radio squawks. Lonnie pauses, cocks his head. Static.

". . . *alive,*" the radio says, in a hoarse whisper.

I see the word register on Lonnie Wayne's face like a ripple on a pond.

Real slow, he turns his head to face all of us, a dozen silent corpses standing mute in the dawn. Spirits who are not alive and not yet dead. Honor-bound to survive.

Lonnie lowers his pistol.

"Still alive," hisses the radio. *"Still alive."*

The old man blinks the low sunlight out of his eyes along with a couple of crystalline tears. Holsters his weapon with trembling hands. My skin can't feel it when he cups my ruined face in his palms. I can't smell him when he pushes his forehead against mine. Inside, though, my heart is stinging with a pure, eternal kind of sadness that never makes it to my face. Never will again.

"We'll get through this, son," he says, simply.

If I could cry, I guess I would do it about now.

Not for what happened to me and my soldiers, or for the bone-tired despair dragging down the bags under Lonnie's eyes. I would cry for something even worse. For the sick orange glow that's been spreading just over the horizon. For what I recognize as the birth of another Archos, its tendrils of control looping and roiling out of a growing evil haze. For the never-ending goddamn trials of living things.

If I could, I'd cry for what's to come.

GOD MODE

Memories. Nauseous snatches of infinity, trickling in, thumbing into my forehead, pinning me to this flower-smelling bed. My fractured thoughts are bursting away with the cannon-shot split of glaciers, broken towers that knife into a sea of amnesia.

In all of this forgetting, there is this one constant thing.

Her name is Sarah. I will always remember that.

She is holding my right hand with her left. Our fingers are interlaced, familiar. The two of us have held hands this way before. The memory of it is there, in our grasp.

Her hand in mine. This is all that matters to me now. Here in the aftermath of the great forgetting.

I'm twenty. Studying abroad at the University of Melbourne in Australia. Today I'm riding on a crowded tram, south to St. Kilda beach.

Sarah.

Another American mixed in among dozens of Aussie college kids in bathing suits and bikinis, all of us packed into the heaving car, bare shoulders kissing as the heat rolls off sticky black plastic floorboards. We are headed to the beach on Christmas holiday.

Her hair is brown streaked with blond. Her lips are red. Teeth white.

The tram pulls to a stop. Double doors accordion open and a cool salty breeze floods in. I'm watching her when she faints. Her eyes roll up and she falls and I try to catch her. But my grip isn't strong enough. She's beautiful and lean and tan under a sheen of sweat. She slips through my grasp and instead of saving her, I leave four bright red scratch marks across her shoulder blades.

Her sun-kissed hair swirls as her head hits the floor.

Sarah is only unconscious for a few seconds. Then her brown eyes are fluttering open and I'm holding her left hand with my right, pulling her up toward me, apologizing to her for the scratches and never for a moment realizing that our lives have now been grafted together, forever.

I remember. I think I can remember.

This is the day that the stars disappeared.

For the rest of the afternoon, Sarah is woozy from the fall. Bright light hurts her eyes, so I'm pulling the plastic rolling shades down over her small dorm window. Outside, downtown Melbourne is babbling to itself. Her room is tiny, just four white-painted concrete walls cradling a college twin-sized bed across from a sink. Drawers are built into the wall. We haven't stopped talking since I pulled Sarah to her feet.

We sit together on sheets that smell like flowers. The sun falls.

Later, we lie whispering in the dark. My bare feet are pressed against the cool wall. Muffled sounds of the dormitory reverberate around us: laughter, drawers slamming, music, the slap of feet on tile floors.

Sarah and I are talking philosophy while the stars blink out one by one, billions of miles away. The rules of physics are splintering and the foundation of rational thinking is dissolving like a half-remembered dream.

Holding hands in bed, we talk.

I can remember now. If I try very hard.

Sarah studies English. I am in Melbourne to study how to make video games. She doesn't blame me for the scratches I left on her back when she fell. She says I was only trying to hold on. Her teeth are so white. The sharp angles of her face are tanned and an unlikely round dimple is tucked into the corner of her cheek.

A few nights later, she leaves scratches on my back.

We are both trying to hold on.

"What's beyond the mountains?" Sarah asks me.

I am building my video game world, hands sweaty on the controller. This is my senior project. I call it "Synthesis." As I create this world, my point of view leaps across valleys and over mountains. I am gazing down on a fractally generated city and all its myriad, faceless inhabitants.

"Nothing," I say.

"Nothing?" she asks. "There must be something."

"If it isn't rendered by the computer, it doesn't exist."

"So . . . if you can't see it, then it isn't there?"

"Right," I say.

"What if you look anyway?" she asks.

"We would see nothing," I repeat. "Well, not nothing. Just . . . gray, I guess."

On the news, they can't stop talking about how the stars are gone.

There are quiet classes and subdued parties and always Synthesis. I lose track. We are reassured that the loss above us is some trick of the universe. Got to be. It's impossible for stars to all disappear out of the sky at the same time. They're different distances away. The light takes different amounts of time to reach us. To disappear at once, they'd all have to have gone supernova at different moments, based on how far away from Earth they were.

That's impossible.

Another day and I'm creating the world again. Sarah tells me I should get a hobby. Play a sport. I tell her that I'm saving my body for old age. If I don't use up my energy now, I say, then I'll have it ready for later. Some people burn the candle at both ends, but I blew mine out. I am saving the wax for my old age.

She laughs and laughs.

In Synthesis, I float through walls. Putting things together, you've got to see all the moving pieces. Sarah sits cross-legged next to me on her bed, wearing knee-length yoga pants and watching me work. She says she likes seeing how the textures roll across the landscape. A flat plane sprouts into a tangled wilderness. A gray cube shivers and grows a brick skin studded with glinting windows.

This is called "God Mode."

It's the act of creation, she says.

It's just a simulation, I say.

You can simulate a nuclear blast on a supercomputer and

nobody gets blown up. You can simulate the birth of a universe but that doesn't make you a god. The simulation is convincing, but it doesn't have the intrinsic quality of the real thing.

The real-realness just isn't there.

"Right?" I ask.

Sarah is quiet for a long time. I have hurt her feelings somehow.

She scoots in behind me on the bed, wrapping her long legs around my waist. Now, she settles her elbows onto my shoulder blades. When she speaks I can feel her lips brushing my neck.

"If you can see it, then it's there," she says. "Even if it's only gray."

After the lights are out, Sarah and I walk up to the roof. Laying beach towels over the scabby asphalt and pebbles, we lie on our backs and peer up into a nothing sky. There are no clouds. No light coming down. Just the light of the city going up.

Like we're at the bottom of a black ocean.

I turn my head and my cheek touches Sarah's. I can feel that her cheek is wet.

Sarah is crying silently to see it. This emptiness.

"It's okay," she says. "I'm just a little scared."

"The scientists can explain it," I say and I don't sound convinced.

We don't go back up to the roof again.

I decide I don't want to see what's beyond the mountains.

They don't cancel classes right away.

The man on the news interviews scientists. They have theories to explain why the stars are gone. An invisible storm of electromagnetic energy, reacting with the atmosphere to block the light. An envelope of gas engulfing the planet. A primordial cloud of matter has floated in from intersolar space and swallowed our solar system.

We cling to the explanations.

I am from Oklahoma. Sarah is from Manhattan. I call home once a month. She calls her mom once a week. And then one day—no more calls.

There is a story about it in the last newspaper.

All the satellites have gone. The government advises people to stay calm and in their homes. Scientists are going to figure this out, they say. The headline is that Australia has lost contact with the other continents.

Classes are canceled after that.

Things are loud in the dormitories for a little while. The walls are so thin. Friends and couples argue. Doors bang open and closed. Bags are packed and dragged down hallways. Sarah and I sit on her bed and we whisper. She keeps the panic from surging up my throat. Her hand is in mine and we squeeze until our fingers are numb. After a little while, things are much quieter.

I bring all of my leftover food and a trash bag full of clothes to Sarah's dorm and I throw it in the corner. We both agree that I should stay here from now on. My roommate was already gone when I went back to my room. He left a note saying that he had decided to head down to the coast to see if there was any news off the boats that dock there.

I don't remember seeing him again.

Sarah and I lie side by side in the dark. The black of no stars has been getting more gray lately. It has been hard to keep track of the time.

"Should we run?" I ask.

"Where would we go?" she asks. "Our families are on the other side of the planet. We're stuck between the desert and an ocean."

The normal things. They used to be so simple. Now, it is so hard to keep track.

"I don't feel hungry," I say.

"Me neither," she says.

"When did we eat last?"

"I don't know," she whispers, and I feel her fingers searching for my hand.

———

Did we run? Did Sarah and I take off across the continent, searching for an explanation? Did we live a life together? I think . . . I can't remember. It always comes back to the dormitory. The most familiar things . . . they always come back to me in the end.

We are lying in Sarah's bed where the sheets smell like flowers, our fingers intertwined. I stand up and I cannot remember how long I have been sleeping. Or whether I was sleeping or just lying, looking at a white ceiling.

"Final stage," says a whisper.

"What?" I ask.

"Nothing," Sarah says, face muffled by her pillow. "I didn't say anything."

I peek out the small window. In the street, I see that a Royal Australian Naval Reserves guard is posted on the intersection. A young blond guy in tan camouflage, sweating under his helmet. The sun is only a golden hint in a gray sky. The soldier is watching the streets. He does not have a shadow.

"Let's go outside," I say to Sarah. "We're sleeping too much."

Sarah and I are walking down Swanston Street. Down the middle of the tram tracks, bright slices of metal curving through clean concrete. The electric wires are shivering overhead, twanging in a nonexistent breeze.

The sky is gray. No more clouds.

"It's quiet," she says, and her words are flat, without an echo.

"Where did the people go?" I ask.

The soldier is gone.

"I don't know," she says. "I don't really remember anyone here very well, anyway."

I turn abruptly and walk down a side street.

The grayness has a way of growing thicker. Details fade. My vision collapses until I am seeing the world from the bottom of a well. I spin and reach for Sarah in a sudden panic.

Her fingers feel hard and real. She pulls me back, our fingertips connecting like antennae, hands curling together into their familiar embrace.

"Are we in a video game?" I ask. "Did I fall asleep?"

"No," she says. "You aren't in a video game. Come back."

In the distance, I see the silhouettes of the campus buildings. But they look strange. Two dimensional.

"Okay," I say.

We walk, our footsteps echoing flatly against the pavement. There is no detail to the cement, anymore. No dark patches of long-chewed gum or pale scratches from skateboards. It's just . . . gray. Like everything.

"I feel like I've known you a long time, Sarah," I say.

"I know," she says, and we walk on.

"That's so odd," she says, after a few moments.

"What?"

"The only thing left out here . . . is the way I walk to campus," she says. "Everything else is just gray."

An apocalypse should be loud. Gunshots and rioting, that kind of thing. Life screaming out to live. But this is quiet. Dark. The gray of forgotten details. The people are just gone. People I never knew. Never will know.

Standing at the dorm window, I watch as the round eye of the sun suddenly spreads out and leaks into light that comes from all directions. The cardboard city outside goes dull. Even flatter, somehow.

And after that, the dark doesn't come again.

Sarah lies on her bed, asleep. She is so clear to me. Her colors are vibrant.

The radius of reality is shrinking, but Sarah is this one constant thing. The curve of her cheek on the pillow is so familiar. How strange that I am twenty. How strange that I have known her for so long in such a short amount of life.

I think we are the last ones living in Sarah's dormitory.

Sometimes I wander through the empty hallways, peek into the rooms.

Before, each room was different. But now they're all the same.

A twin bed across from a sink. A whining fluorescent light. Always on, flickering. Wooden drawers built into the wall and a gray square of glass.

"I don't know if the campus is really there anymore," I say to Sarah, and panic is building in my throat. "It's just this room. It's just us."

Her hand closes onto mine.

My thoughts are lazy ripples through still water. The realization comes slow, like mist evaporating off a pond.

Sarah is the dreamer.

We lost the stars on the day she hit her head. The more she sleeps, the more we lose. The gray of her forgetting is eating the world. Now, only her strongest memories are alive. The walk to class. This room. Me.

I move closer to her sleeping body, press myself against her.

This morning—*morning, is there such a thing anymore*—I walk to the front door of the dormitory and I look out and I see that the sky is missing. A postbox is on its side in the street, half-buried in the pavement. The red metal skin of it is juddering on and off. Between the blinks I can see mail inside.

Before I go back upstairs, I put my hand on the glass of the door and it doesn't feel cool. It doesn't feel warm, either. It doesn't feel like anything.

Sarah is curled on her bed. Shaking. She is shaking and moaning.

I hold her, feel her hair slithering over my arms.

The world outside is getting smaller.

Sarah shakes. The forgetting grows.

I don't remember waking up. I am floating in gray. My body is falling through the walls and it's so familiar.

I am holding Sarah in my arms and I can feel the cool sand of the beach under my hip. I am stroking her sea-smelling hair and murmuring into the soft dampness. "It will be okay," I'm saying. "You're the dreamer, Sarah."

"We can find each other in your dreams," I say to her.

And then the smell of her hair is gone, along with the feel of the sand. I open my eyes to look down at my body and I am tumbling, spinning in space because I have no eyes. There is no body. All of it has finally gone away.

Things unseen are not rendered.

And yet I am still here.

I am thinking. My thoughts are somewhere. Churning in the gray.

Sarah slipped through my fingers.

Was she my dream, then?

Am I the dreamer?

———

Even now, there is this one constant thing.

A pressure where my hand should be.

Fingers, laced into mine. Squeezing.

I can remember if I try very hard.

"Final stage." I hear the whisper.

Something beats at my eyes. A flutter of reality. A line of hard light appears and shatters my vision into a briar's patch of eyelashes.

I am opening my eyes.

And I find myself lying in a flower-smelling bed under a clean white ceiling that is chopped into neat squares. There is a gray video screen hanging on the wall.

"Final stage," says that unfamiliar voice. "Neural calibration and transmission complete."

Sarah?

Eyes swiveling down, I see that my right hand is a leathery claw, laced with blue-black veins, knuckles twisted and humped.

A small moan comes from my dry, cracked throat.

I am old. I am ancient. *I am twenty how am I twenty?*
And my Sarah.

She is lying next to me on the bed—*it's a hospital bed this isn't right where is our dorm?* Her lips are peeled back into a sweet worried smile and I can see a hint of that beauty I remember in her youthful angular face—a dimple still lodged stubbornly in her sagging cheek.

We are . . . old. Melted like wax.

I was saving my wax. I blew out my candle. I was twenty.

Years have draped themselves over us. Did we fall asleep?

"I lost you," I say.

"No," she whispers. "We're together now. Forever."

The screen on the wall flickers, shows me something painful.

Sarah and I are standing together on the screen.

Versions of us. In the computer.

We are holding hands and smiling.

It makes me cry to see us so young.

"Neural upload complete," says the voice in the gray. "Both computational entities are viable. It's a success, people."

I think the world is running away between my blinks. The screen and the ceiling and the walls are splitting off and falling into the great forgetting.

Only she is vibrant.

"Hosts are losing mental cohesion," says a gray whisper.

Sarah.

She is lying next to me on her back with tears tracing down her temple. Our fingers have found their old familiar places. Her face is so bright that it hurts my eyes. Her lips are red again. Her hair is a sun-kissed brown.

We are both trying so hard to hold on.

"Sarah?" I ask.

"I'm not scared anymore," she says and her teeth are so white. "It will be okay. We'll find each other in our dreams."

Her hand in mine. It's all that matters.

In all of this forgetting, there is this one constant thing.

Her name is Sarah. I will always remember that.

GARDEN OF LIFE

The garden of life is complex, way beyond the ken of humankind. Textbooks say science has only stumbled upon around 10 percent of all existing species of plants and animals. There could be from 10 to 100 million more. Critters, big and small (mostly small), are living and reproducing and dying as they have for eternity . . . without a human being ever so much as laying eyes on them.

It's a wide old world out there for a taxonomist.

There are more living things hidden in the wilds than we'll ever know. Life likes to break free and spread. And what you can find will surprise you.

I'm on what I call one of my long jaunts. A jaunt is supposed to be short by definition, but I enjoy the paradox.
In fact, I enjoy it just about every weekend and holiday.
Come Saturday morning, I pull on my hiking boots, tuck
my pant legs into them, and lace them up tight. Out here
in the mountains, there's a particular area that's all mine to
explore. Miles of government land surrounding some kind
of research center. Scrubby deer trails meandering through
scalp-prickling heat. Tick-infested pine trees and plenty of
poison ivy. But every now and then, you'll find a cool hollow. Caves gouged out of sweating granite. Plenty of micro-
climates are hiding there in the rough country, off the horse
trails and way aways from where idiot four-wheelers scream
and churn mud.

Worse it is out here, the better I like it.

Some people get a thrill jumping from a plane. Out on
the lake, kids'll get those wakeboards going faster than I'm
comfortable driving my Chevy half-ton on the highway.
That's not for me. I get my jollies in the wild, hunting for
brand-new insect species. I send my specimens to an old
buddy at the university's entomology department, then play
the waiting game. Sometimes, I hit pay dirt . . . and then
comes the best part: I get to name them.

Gryllus oklahomas was my last find. A field cricket under
a piece of rotten bark. Named that little dude in honor of
my state and kept on looking for more.

I find the fist-sized knot in the base of a dead pine tree.
Sort of a cubbyhole in the shape of a stop sign. The little

hexagon has too many straight lines to be from nature, so I stoop down on creaking knees and take a look.

The smell of burning wood wafts from the hole. Peering into the thing, I see that it holds what looks like a plastic cube with an ember in it. And around the lip of the hexagonal hole, I see a brownish leg that is moving in precise jerks. It has a claw tip and it's busy scratching . . . building something. Staring at it for a second, I realize it's making another little arm, a perfect copy of itself.

"What in the . . . ," I ask the empty woods.

When I was a kid, I used to find fairy nests near the creek that ran behind my parents' place. Little shacks made of sticks and moss and leaves, placed around a shade tree or in a sun-dappled clearing. In those days, kids roamed free, and I spent a whole summer hunting those fairy nests with a kind of magic in my heart. One night at dinner, I finally told my mama about what I'd found. I will always remember the little smile she gave me. All of a sudden I knew exactly where those fairy houses came from.

I knew, but I never stopped searching.

Something tickles my hand and I give a yelp. In the dirt, I see a handful of marbles. Only they're moving on lots of legs, like pill bugs, or roly-polies, as we once called them. The insects are trundling and falling over a piece of bark, peeling splinters from the wood. The size of thimbles, each one has a raspy spot on its belly. They drag themselves over the wood and shred little pieces off. I watch one pick up a splinter with tiny mandibles and climb right into the hexagonal hole.

He's tending the fire in there. Keeping energy going to his factory.

This is a whole new deal. I climb onto my knees and rifle through my field bag. Pick up one of the little crawlers with tweezers and drop it into a glass specimen jar. I screw the lid on tight and wonder if it really needs airholes. Can't say whether this little dude breathes or not. For the life of me, it looks like the bug is made of some kind of *metal*.

Government land, you know? Hard to say what the scientists are doing in those fenced-off buildings. Only thing I know is that life likes to break free.

Life likes to spread.

Getting to my feet, I shade my eyes and look deeper into the woods. Now, I notice a lot of the trees are dead. More than usual. And it may just be my old eyes, but I feel like there's a haze over everything. A thin smear of smoke from more of those miniature power plants . . . more smoldering factories out there in the sunbaked woods.

I stand still, and the movement of the crawlers seeps into view. Thousands of them, the color of dirt and leaves, dragging themselves like a living carpet over the ground. The hair goes up on the backs of my arms. Somewhere out there, far off, I hear a tree splinter and crack. A shadow sweeps and I hear a hollow thump.

The captured crawler clinks against its jar and I flinch a little bit. Time to get back to the truck. I shrug my pack on tighter and turn around. And even though I start out walking at a reasonable pace . . . before long I'm running.

In the truck, I don't take it easy on the accelerator. I'm

on a dirt road for a few miles, meandering alongside razor-wire fences. My tires chew the rocks loudly, and I can't see anything but my dust trail in the rearview, which is fine with me. When I finally stop at the sign to get onto paved road, it gets quiet except for my ragged breathing. I'm gripping the steering wheel, knuckles like mountain ridges.

Then I hear the scratching sound from next to me.

Fingers shaking, I swipe all the trash off the passenger seat. A curled yellow newspaper, a pair of work gloves, and an *Auto Trader* magazine waterfall onto the floorboard. Underneath, I find more of my friends-with-no-names. Guess I must have left my window open while I was exploring the woods. The crawlers are busy making themselves right at home, pulling strips of fabric out of the seat back.

They're carving out a neat hexagon shape.

I take a deep breath and put my foot on the gas. A shaky smile has got onto my face. The garden of life, see . . . she's way beyond the ken of humankind. The textbooks say we've barely scratched the surface. At the first exit, I head off toward the university. I'm pretty sure these bugs are made of metal, and I'm pretty sure they were built and not born. But if nature doesn't care, then neither do I.

I'm already thinking of names.

ALL KINDS OF PROOF

Joe is a misanthrope and a drunk.

I never did take to cigarettes, you know. Or any of the ones after them. Vaping. E-cigs. Charged burners. There's always an electronic version of everything these days. A sparkling paint job plastered over the same old shit. The suits have gotta move merchandise somehow, I guess. But I never took to any of it.

What happens with me is whenever somebody tries to convince me of something, my gut reaction is a big old *"fuck you, buddy."*

Head down and I'm moving on, you understand. Keep the change.

If there's some kind of an organization to whatever-it-is, then just forget about it. And that goes for everything. Religion. Sports. A job.

Hell, especially the job side of things.

You learn a little bit about yourself after five or six decades. And I know I'm mostly built to be solitary, in that I can handle about one other human being. Two at most and then only when I was young. And despite every goddamn Hollywood movie, I don't think a person can help the way they're built. You can't change what's in your heart or grow a pair of balls all of a sudden. For chrissake, just be honest with yourself and get on with living your life. Maybe try and do the best you can for the ones you do care about.

I tend to think about this kind of garbage while I'm sitting outside the Goose, not smoking cigarettes, staring down my first whiskey and beer back of the day. Something to get my eyes open in the early afternoon, is all.

And if you're judging me, you should see the other regulars.

My spot is on the front sidewalk of the Goose Hill Bar & Grill, alone at a rickety table next to a dented dog bowl that the bartender, Mallory, sometimes remembers to fill with water. I'm about a foot from the curb and usually on the verge of getting my neck snapped by a side-view mirror. Through an open window, I can see the barflies who sit inside. At the moment Sherry, the back of her neck tattooed with spiderwebs, is lighting up the place with her cackle. Adrian, an aging busker in a purple beret, is hee-hawing right along with her. She really is the queen of the bar, holding court to that fawning group of well-lubricated drunks.

Mallory pours them strong, God bless her, and that's why we're all here.

I can smell the stale cigarette smoke wafting around the corner of the building. The bums who sit over there in the smoking section—I can't see them, can only hear their occasional shouting matches—are coughing down butts plucked from the sidewalk after a long day scrounging and begging. They're literally bums over there, you know? It's not just a turn of phrase or petty name-calling on my part.

Good for the bums, though. Any one of us could end up around that corner, quicker than we might suspect. At least they're enjoying themselves.

Up the other way are a bunch of metal pigs.

They've got a name that I forget. But the three sculptures are fat and silver and bolted to the sidewalk, just the right size for kids to climb around on until they fall off and get hurt. Which they nearly always do. The pigs are wearing chains around their necks with their names on them. And at their feet is a homemade lockbox, welded together out of solid steel with a rolling tube for dropping money inside. A shitty piece of half-laminated, half-soaked paper is taped to it: "Donations."

It seems like such an obvious scam I can't believe how many people jam coins and bills inside the thing, you know?

Every few days, the dude we call Hemingway comes shuffling out of the Goose with a few leaves of curled-up newspaper in his gnarled fingers. He wears a navy blue flat cap and a beard as white as sea spray. He must be in his late seventies, but the old reprobate still has twinkling blue eyes and the swagger of a twenty-year-old.

Hemingway.

It takes him a few minutes, but he'll toss down his papers, crouch to unlock the box, and then dump and scrape the money out onto the newspaper. He rolls it up, takes it inside, and my guess is he gives it straight to Mallory to pay his tab. It happens quiet and on a regular schedule and nobody says a thing about it.

Those shining pigs are dumb and mute and they're a lifeline for the old bastard.

I see it all from my perch. The folks here mostly give me space to myself and that's fine. I'm not clubby. In case you hadn't guessed, my preference is to observe.

So, yeah, that means I enjoy watching the angular girls in clunky glasses that come clip-clopping past. The kind with soft eyes and sharp hips—who send a snap of endorphins thrashing through a man's brain at the speed of a grunt.

But that's not what I mean by observe.

What I'm trying to talk about is all those things we see and yet we don't see. Like the kid wearing a sagging back-pack and his straightlaced customer, walking side by side, making their exchange in a subtle clasp of hands; or the elderly guy reaching into an open car window and snatching a jacket off the seat; or maybe it's something more altruistic, like a shopkeep dropping a pair of old boots next to some sorry lump in a sleeping bag.

It's those little times. Those fleeting moments when people don't expect a reward or a punishment. I enjoy bearing witness to them.

Because things are happening, you know? And what I really mean to say by that is things are *going down*. And, more clearly, *shit* is going down, all around us, all the time, on any street.

Even on these wet Portland streets.

So that's my thing. I sit in the flow for a couple days or months, years or decades. Watch the shadows creep over the pavement and the shoes traipse back and forth. And after a while, I'm grown into a place like a tree through a chain-link fence.

The world is pretty goddamn interesting, if you look at it long enough. Have a little patience and imagination. You wait for something to happen, and if it doesn't, why then you wait some more.

My problem with it is—a guy can only go it alone for so long. I don't need much, but I'm sure as hell no island. I get lonely, like anybody. And in life I think most of us need a confidant. Nothing magical, just somebody to swap conversation and arguments and complaints with, pulling the words out of each other like snake-poisoned blood.

A person needs company. And it's not often you find a pal like the one I had.

Old Shining Armor, the son of a bitch. Called him Shiny, or the Shine. He's a rare one. Tight-lipped and loyal. Sun Tzu said don't ever hang out with degenerates, they'll pull you down. And he was right. But it cuts both ways. You end up with somebody like the Shine around you—somebody with no guile and no bullshit; only the truth, and a simple truth at that—and you can't help but return the favor and be a little better than you are.

That's assuming you're any kind of decent human being anyway, which most of us aren't. Maybe especially not me.

But I never let him down, you know?

Never smoked, and I never let the Shine down. Not even when fists were flying and my boss fat Dave, that fucking tomato, was frothing at the mouth, crashing his post office duty van over the sidewalk under the Fremont Bridge with the bums and urchins scattering like crows around a highway carcass.

I stuck with my old pal through all of it, let me tell you.

Joe gets a job.

Me and Shine met on the job. Coworkers, if you want to call it that. We were assigned together, or I guess I was assigned to him—to look after him, you see? The Shine is simple and that's the beautiful thing about him, but he's also easily confused. Blind, half the time. Too dumb to ask questions and lost more often than not. Shining Armor has good instincts, but he needs a caretaker.

So that's me.

I'm out on a rainy afternoon with a six-pack of tallboy Rainiers under my arm, a spring in my step, the goods wrapped in a brown paper bag like a Christmas present. Walking past the post office, I see this fella wearing a fuzzy red sweater like it had been knit straight around him, tighter than a sausage casing. He's a real little guy but fat, panting even, a beard clinging to his face like a chinstrap while he struggles to staple a flyer to a telephone pole.

Slowing, I can't tell what has him so heated up. It's sort of raining, just spitting really, and the afternoon is bruised and brooding. My favorite kind of day.

So I go ahead and ask the red balloon what about it, and the guy invites me right in for an interview. Says he's hiring for the easiest job in the world. Any sucker can do it. That sounds like me, so I follow him into the main post office, across those squeaky polished floors from a 1950s high school and into a cramped office lit up under a fluorescent tube like the devil's night-light.

"You really want to hire me?" I ask him.

"We're hiring anybody who'll take the job," he says.

"Delivering mail?"

"Yeah," he says, with an evil smirk. "Delivering the mail."

I'm sort of intrigued. Perched on the edge of my chair, I wind up and take a breath and get all ready to explain away the DUIs and the rest of the record, to try to laugh them off, which never works but I have to at least try. But the furry mound says this doesn't involve driving—just a whole lot of walking. And I sure as hell get excited then because I think that's terrific. I'm a born walker. My whole family has long shanks, and I don't care about the weather either. Living in Portland you've got to be waterproof. All kinds of proof, pretty much.

He shoves over an employment contract stuck to a clipboard.

But now I'm picking up on how the guy is acting kind of snide. He's laughing at the light in my eyes, trying to sound convincing but laughing at *me,* really. And I start to get it that he thinks I'm dumb. Which is fine, why should I care what he thinks of my intelligence or lack of it? This guy—"Dave," I see now, because he's wearing a name tag on his sweater—he's no captain of industry. But the thing that worries me is how he seems to have this in-joke, like I was signing up for the army and a war just broke out.

I sign anyway. Fuck it. Nobody much is offering me jobs.

"How old are you, chief?" he asks.

"Old enough, *Dave,*" I say, and he shakes his head.

"You look older than that," he says.

Ah, well, fuck him. I shrug and pick up my sack of beers.

"Good luck with your flyers," I say, showing him my back.

He laughs once, kind of in disbelief. But before I can book it out of there, I hear his desk drawer grate open. There's this thunk and a rattle as I walk out the door.

"Here, you're gonna need this," he says.

Oh boy.

I just gotta turn around to see, so I drop the prima donna act. And there on his desk, I swear to God, is a *leash*.

"That's in your hand eight hours a day, five days a week until you quit or get fired," he says.

Now old Dave has got my gears turning. I'm not thinking about those cold tall ones for the first time in a long time. I'm keen now, looking to find out what's got the crimson spud so hot and sweaty.

I pick up the leash and turn it over in my rough hands. It's a silver coil, real futuristic. Some kind of attachment at the end, with little pins in it like the cables people sometimes use to charge their lumps of black glass at the bar.

"So what the hell is this for?" I ask.

"Not what," says Dave, smirking again, his double chin eating that chinstrap beard like a free buffet. "It's *who*."

I can already tell Dave's going to be a dick of a boss. And right then I almost toss the leash down and go. I am actually starting to crave one of those beers sweating in the paper sack, and plus I know I don't have the patience to make sure this ends well.

So I give him one more second. And that's enough.

"C'mon," says Dave, standing up.

I follow the chicken nugget down a cramped hallway into a beat-up little storage room. There's cardboard shreds strewn everywhere, dotted with packing peanuts like croutons, as if somebody unpacked something with some anger.

And that's how I meet the Shine. Isn't that terrific?

He's standing there in the middle of the room, wavering a bit on his sturdy steel legs—a little slope-shouldered fellow with a face like a transistor radio. He stands up to about my midsection on backward ostrich legs and he smells like a warm battery, kind of humming to himself.

"A friggin' robot?" I ask.

"Bipedal mail delivery unit," reads Dave off a piece of paper, scowling as he brushes packing peanuts off its metal-plated dome. "USPS is testing them out, seeing if they can't find a new kind of postman."

"You seem thrilled."

"You picking up on that?" he says, voice rising. "This piece of crap is going to take my job. As soon as it learns the city routes. And that's why I have to hire somebody like you to lead him around by the nose until he can map the neighborhood. It could take six months. It could take a year. But the writing is on the wall."

Somebody like me, huh? Right then, I decide I love the little piece of crap.

Kneeling down, I let my fingers skim over the robot's plastic face. The metal casing over his shoulders and thighs is gleaming silver and warm. He has short little arms with flat hands like mittens. A blunt peg is sticking out of his back, for hanging a mail bag on, I figure. His eyes are round and glossy black. He blinks at me slow with a little click.

I think he's handsome, like an old hound dog. But a lot shinier.

"Like a little knight in shining armor," I say, but Dave

doesn't hear me. He's muttering to himself, sweating rivers under that ridiculous sweater. And right then, I get the queer feeling this little fella standing here is the harbinger of big things to come.

Joe and the Shine become good friends, and inseparable.

So here's the deal with the Shine—he doesn't judge, doesn't interrupt, and he goes with me everywhere. When he walks, it makes this nice wheezing sound. His narrow little feet are coated in a layer of tacky rubber and each step lands quiet and smooth. And he always keeps up.

The two of us walk together, a lot, and we make quite a goddamn sight.

Everybody is on about the drones to deliver everything. And hell, maybe they're okay for the suburbs and the country. But in the city, there's no spot for those things to land with all the trees and power lines and buildings.

It's a hoof-it-or-bust proposition when you're downtown.

Technically, Shine is a postman, but he doesn't carry any mail. Not yet. Dave says he's being trained, and the most important thing for him is to memorize every route at all different times, in all different weather, and with all the different changes of scenery that come along across the year. Plus, the eggheads are looking for what they call "outliers"—all the crazy shit that wasn't likely to happen and yet it did.

That's pretty much my specialty.

I take the Shine with me everywhere, and we observe. I show him the patterns that I love—the flow of the shop-keepers, the tourists, and bums. The way the leaves form waving shadows on the sidewalks and how the new LED streetlamps shatter their light into grids of glowing squares. Even the traffic.

He soaks it up, and I flatter myself that he appreciates it.

I can hear what you're thinking, all right? And look, I get that he's a machine. Not even that smart of one, except he's pretty good at walking. But I don't care. I'm not a judgmental type of guy. If the itch is scratched, I'm happy. And striding through the city with the Shine on my heels, his leash tucked through one of my belt loops—well, it makes me happy. It's just satisfying, to have somebody by your side.

So maybe you think there's something sad about that. But there isn't. And besides, you're free to screw off any-time. Nobody's keeping you here.

Lucky for me, Dave doesn't care when the miles get logged, so long as they do. Meaning I'm free to keep to my regular schedule of walking in the mornings and day drinking. And even better, a couple weeks in I discover a compartment over the Shine's hip. Like a glove box. It's just big enough for a flask of Jameson. From there, you can predict how things went with me and the Shine.

We spend a lot of time together at the Goose.

People stop and gawk every now and then. Sometimes

they take pictures of him, like he's a really pretty dog. At some point, some kids slap their skateboard stickers on him while I'm taking a leak or grabbing another round. And he falls once or twice, collecting some scrapes and scars like the rest of us.

The Goose regulars each have their own reaction, or nonreaction.

Old Hemingway shuffles out the wooden front door of the Goose with his curled-up newspaper pages and his hearing aids. He looks at the robot, looks at me, and shakes his head. Keeps going right past and on to tend to his piggies.

Sherry—her majesty, the queen of the Goose—is the one who doesn't care for the Shine. She roosts next to her husband in the soaking grotto at the end of the bar, joking and bullshitting with her crowd: Adrian the busker, old Hemingway, Mallory (who's there as a captive audience), and whatever ragtag reprobates have straggled in.

Sherry sits in front of a tall glass of grapefruit and vodka. Mostly vodka, honestly. She's got a figure like an hourglass with football pads on. That may not sound good, but it's all right. She's also got this nice cackle that kind of punctuates the babble of drunken talking that goes on in there.

The windows are always open, so I hear what they say, even though it usually washes over me as pure sound without meaning. Which it mostly is, anyway.

But from my spot to her spot, it's only about ten feet.

The way I figure it, our getting together was pretty much inevitable. Proximity, you know?

So it's too bad Sherry doesn't take to the Shine. Not at all.

She likes to keep all the attention to herself, as it turns out, and if she had her way she'd knock him to hell with a wrench. From my point of view, the Shine can't help attracting some notice. But she doesn't see it that way. Stealing her spotlight, you see?

So, she takes to scowling at us through the window. Which is okay by me, I guess. There are a lot of cackling fish in the sea, so to speak. And even some without husbands.

Joe and the Shine witness a crime.

The day everything goes to shit starts like any other.

I roll out of bed at the crack of dawn and hump it over to the post office back lot. Usually, I'll sneak a quick beer from the minifridge in my apartment or, if it's cold out, a flask of some liquid fire to warm me up. But today is going to be a nice summer day, the sky still pink, so I'm content with smelling the chlorophyll and enjoying the gentle sounds of the city waking up.

Hoofing it all the time, you learn the ins and outs of where to go, depending on what you're looking for. If you're in the mood to see young people with different colors of hair and a little baby fat still clinging to their cheeks, riding bikes without the blessing of gears and going through the motions of being adults—why, walk past the art school. You want to see the new moms and their puppies and babies and round rear-ends wrapped in the most advanced materials known to man, well, that's the Pearl. And if you're in the mood to see the truth, or hell, just to see somebody who isn't doing as well as you, even if you're headed back to a creaking old empty apartment where the dish bowl for a cat who died three years ago is still lying out, well, those some-bodies live in a stripe of shadow under the Fremont Bridge.

What kills me is how young they are. You'd think the folks who've struck out would be older—the haggard types. But no, those ones have got it figured out by now. Those old slobs are all at the Goose or doing a route between Mike's Cellar and Yore's and the Black Jack. Letting them-selves down slow, one step at a time.

People can get good at anything, you know? Even losing.

No, the ones I find under the bridge are mostly kids. Urchins, really, who still think they have something to prove. The weight of that bridge hasn't crushed their souls down into fine powder yet—they're still in the middle of it, and it's a rocky time.

I don't walk that way much.

The post office parking lot is abandoned this early, a sprawl of blue-black asphalt and dirty warehouses and rick-ety old mail trucks. The place is a throwback to when this neighborhood was an industrial wasteland. Then it got trendy. And then less trendy. But it's always been where the big postal trucks root around like groaning dinosaurs—all chain link and exhaust and dark puddles reflecting gray skies.

The Shine has his own room behind a metal rolltop gate. Dave gave me the key, if you can believe that. It was even kind of touching. The first key any employer ever trusted me with. I'm starting to think the gray hair I'm sprouting is giving me some kind of a gravitas. I never earned it or wanted it, but I'll take it.

Anyway, I yank up that gate and there's the Shine, all plugged in and ready to go.

"How about a little nip?" I ask him.

I pat him down and take a pull off the flask that I keep in his hip pocket. Then I toss it back inside and slam his compartment shut. Snap the leash onto his shoulder and drop it through my belt loop and we set off legging it down the street.

"What do you want to do today?" I ask.

He gives me that blank puppy dog look.

"You read my mind, Shine." I wink at him.

We do a long silent loop through the hillside neighborhoods before I finally slide into my usual spot outside the Goose, feeling the sun pushing fingers through the tree that leans out here with me. Up and down the sidewalk, tourists are coming out in full force. I can't remember when they started showing up, exactly. But here they are, filtering through the neighborhood like ants over a picnic. Snapping pictures of the place like they were at Disneyland, and I'm playing the role of a lamppost.

God, but they love those pigs.

The big metal sculptures are bolted to the ground a few feet away from me. On summer days like this, people are jamming cash into the things hand over fist. Pretty good haul for old Hemingway, and I'll bet he can do more than pay his bar tab with it. Between us, I think he really even donates some of that cash.

The old man hobbles out right on schedule and tosses his papers down. Kneels and unlocks the box and empties out the bills and change. He's doing his thing just like clockwork. Problem is, when you've got money lying on the sidewalk for long enough a certain type of person will notice.

A kid is slouching toward us on a BMX bike that's been spray-painted black and scabbed over with duct-taped repairs. He's wearing a backward ball cap and a black bandana over his face, sort of like an outlaw. Whatever he's up to isn't great, but me and Hemingway move too slow to react. Kids like this are living life at twice our speed, flitting around like hummingbirds.

Interesting to watch—scary even—but tiring.

When you can't help but move slow, you learn to just relax and accept whatever the hell is going on. And this time around, what's going on is that Hemingway and his pigs are getting robbed.

Another urchin comes around the smoking corner, also with a bandana on his face. And this one has a knife gleaming in his hand. He's waving his arms, young, shaking with adrenaline, eyes wide and scared over the bandana.

"Give it," he says, as his friend pops the curb and rolls up behind.

Old Hemingway just sighs.

Slowly, he manages to stand back up. With one hand, he makes a dismissive gesture at the wad of bills spilling out of the box like stuffing from a torn couch. Greedy, the kids drop to their knees and start stuffing bills into the pockets of their hoodies.

The Shine and I just sit and watch. Real heroes.

Some faces are appearing in the Goose window—the shadowed, washed-out figures of drunks in a Greek chorus. They're relishing the excitement, buzzing with it, and I know I'll hear their feverish conversations about this for weeks. Deeper inside, Mallory has her piece of plastic up against her head, elbows thrust out, calling the police with barely any interest.

And as the urchins stand up, I see Hemingway's eyes tighten. The old man leans into a tight right hook and catches a kid upside the head, unaware. It knocks the kid's hoodie off and he stumbles back in shock.

"Ow!" he whines.

Snatching his bandana off his face, the kid touches his eye tenderly, glaring at the old man where he stands huffing and puffing.

"Why'd you *do* that?! Fuck!"

The kid wheels around and looks right at me and the Shine, a hurt expression on his face, the beginnings of a beard and mustache tracing dirty lines around his mouth and under his nose. I realize he's looking for sympathy. Christ.

Kids these days.

"C'mon," says his friend, grabbing his elbow.

The urchin hops on the back of his friend's bike, holding his face with one hand and his friend's shoulder with the other.

"You're a dick!" he calls halfheartedly over his shoulder, as the getaway driver pedals furiously, headed toward the river and the bridge.

Hemingway watches them go, breathing hard, fists clenched, a little smile hooked into the corner of his mouth.

Joe sleeps with a married woman.

Like I said, shit is going down all the time. Sometimes I watch it go down, and other times I'm more involved. Like with Sherry.

She started out with careful looks and moved on to suggestive conversations—the close kind, where the other person is watching your lips the whole time. One day I asked her if she was trying to get me into trouble and she said "a little bit."

That seemed like the right amount to me.

Don't get me wrong—Sherry's husband is a nice guy. I don't feel for him, exactly, but I don't *not* feel for him either, you know? He's older than me, always in fleece and tinted glasses and wearing half a grin, like maybe he doesn't understand quite what's going on. Or maybe he just can't hear that great. He's the only one in the bar who actually watches the television. I've seen him sitting and watching, eyes shining, his back hunched like a kid on Saturday morning.

Jaws is on, he'll say to nobody. *Pretty Woman. The Terminator.* Sort of endearing, especially because he passes on watching sports. Which I can respect.

So anyway, Mr. Nice Guy isn't a very observant type. He never perks to it when I give Sherry a little squeeze as I pass by. Or vice versa. Of course, Mallory knew what was going on the day after I first let anything happen. So it's a good thing bartenders the world around know better than to talk about people's business.

That's the only way they keep this whole thing from exploding.

Sherry and Mr. Nice Guy have an apartment above the Goose. It's only a little place but right in the middle of the neighborhood, which is good. It makes it a lot easier to sneak up every now and then, to grab a little more than a squeeze.

So there I am, sitting outside with the Shine, just shooting the shit with him, when I see her pale face peeking through the window. She glares at the Shine, but then her eyes are on me and those painted-on eyebrows are dancing up and down. Even a dope like me can figure out what's on her mind.

Problem is the Shine doesn't do stairs very well, and he's real loud going up and down them. I'm not trying to draw attention to this whole tryst situation, especially with all the chattering crows perched on their bar stools. Sherry comes out and walks past, not even throwing a glance my way. She unlocks her front door and stomps up the wooden steps, leaving it cracked open behind her.

"Shine, buddy," I say. "I've got to see a duchess about a new suit."

The Shine turns to me, kind of sad-looking with stickers all on him. But I gotta get up there while the getting is good. I stand and glance around.

Up the block, I see Adrian perched on the corner with his guitar and his purple beret. The busker is a short guy with long graying hair, probably used to be handsome, but now he's nearly as old as I am, and worse, buried under the layers of coats and scarves and shit you've got to keep on you if you've got no place to leave them. The guy can play that guitar though—enough to hit the Goose at four o'clock and pay his tab when it closes every night. I doubt he's got a home, but the busker doesn't show it in how he stands or talks.

"Adrian, buddy," I'm calling, putting on a big shit-eating grin and pulling the Shine along behind me toward the street corner. I seem to have already got this decision made, even though I'm not sure where exactly my thinking is coming from.

"Can you do me and my friend Jack Daniel's a little favor?" I ask.

A little scowl flashes over his face at the interruption, but then I guess he gets it. The busker puts on a grin as wide and fake as mine.

"Anything for Jack," he says.

Then Adrian holds the leash for me while I head upstairs.

Joe and Sherry argue about the Shine.

Sherry's ready to go in her little apartment. But first she has to pick at me, like any woman does. And if you want to get into bed with her then you shut up and take the ribbing, like any man does. But this time she hits me on my weak spot.

She hits me on the Shine, telling me it's him or her.

"Goddamn it, Sherry," I'm explaining. "The Shine is no threat to anybody. He's dumb as a bag of hammers and twice as ugly. He's got nothing to do with you. I swear to God, what kind of an insecure person—"

"He's a machine, Joe," she says. "I'm a woman. I'm made of flesh and blood—"

And malice and jealousy. Shine's a damn sight more human than she'll ever be.

"Then think of me, why don't you? He means something to me."

"What? What's that robot to you? Compared to me?"

"He's my—"

Friend? Nah, she'll jump on that like a nuke on a Pacific atoll.

"He's my job, you understand?"

"Is that why you spend all afternoon drinking with him? *Talking* to him?"

"Yeah, Sherry. I'm a workaholic," I say, bursting into laughter. "I'm a goddamn workaholic and you knew that about me from the start."

And now she giggles too, in spite of herself, putting a hand over her mouth like a little girl. And whatever else there is about her, I've got to admit she's wide at the top, thin in the middle, and damn wide at the bottom. I can tell she's half-drunk already, and as usual, so am I.

"Come here, goddamn it," I say, pulling on her.

I take Sherry in my arms, fingers settling over the ridge where her bra strap cuts into her fleshy back. Pulling her close, she turns her head and rests her cheek on my shoulder, curly black hair tickling my chin. I feel her big doughy breasts mashing against my chest in a way that makes my crotch tight.

"You're jealous of a robot," I say to her.

Her hand steals down between us and settles in a good spot.

"I'll think about laying off the Shine," she murmurs. "But you got to trade me something."

"Anything you want, darling," I murmur.

The Shine goes missing.

Sherry hits the street first and I wait in the cool stairwell a couple minutes so we're not seen leaving together. Pretty much grade-school-level espionage, but we've got to at least pay lip service to this thing. Besides, it makes it more fun.

Stepping out on the street, I'm feeling warm and cold, a little pang of regret, sure, but mostly just satisfaction at a job well done. Whistling, hands jammed in my pockets, I lean against the wall and wish I smoked. The afternoon rolls by for a few minutes, slow and golden. Bits of cottonwood fluff are floating down the hill from Forest Park. Cars are flickering like minnows through creek water.

It's nice there for a minute, is what I'm trying to say.

Then I get a bad feeling. The corner is empty. No Adrian. And no Shine.

"Oh goddamn it," I mutter.

I turn and beeline for the Goose. The front door is propped wide open and I round the corner hot, blinking in the sudden gloom, my hands clenching and unclenching.

The Shine's my job and my friend, you see, and I'm worried about him.

That goddamned dirty bum, Adrian, is across the room, leaning in his chair against the railing with his arms laid out like it's the crucifixion, a battered guitar case at his feet. He's got his amber whiskey poured already and his unlaced boots propped up on a chair. The son of a bitch is laughing at something.

The phone behind the bar is ringing, ignored, as usual.

Sherry's at the counter, leaning on her elbows, eyes wide under her black mess of curly hair as she watches me pass. The look on my face must not be very nice.

"Adrian," I urge. "Buddy, where's the Shine?"

"Huh?" he says.

It's the single most infuriating word in the history of the English language, or hell, any language that doesn't involve clicks or hieroglyphics.

"The robot I left you with," I repeat. "Where is he?"

"Oh," he says. "Shit, man. I thought you knew I was high."

"You're high," I say.

"I'm . . . *high,*" he says, bursting into giggles.

My fists come unclenched. I knew better. That's the bitch of it, especially when you've been around and supposed to have learned something about life and the degenerates who populate it. I knew better, and I left the Shine to go get laid.

Behind the bar, the phone is still ringing like a godforsaken fire alarm.

Adrian sees my face and leans forward. He's real earnest now, like he's got an important message.

"Hey, Joe," he says. "I did see something."

In an exaggerated motion, he nods toward Sherry.

"What?" I ask.

He nods his head at her again, nearly falling off his chair.

"What?!" I exclaim over the ringing of that goddamn phone.

This time he does tumble off his chair, laughing. Climbs to his feet like a drunk in the surf and now I go ahead and leave him.

Sometimes you need a second to regenerate your ability to deal with people. I'm headed out the door to try and find that when Mallory calls to me. She's finally answered the phone, receiver pressed to her collarbone.

"Your boss is calling for you from the post office, Joe," she says.

Dave. Great.

"I'm not here," I say, headed out the door.

"He's in a panic. He wants to know what's going on with the Shine," says Mallory.

"I'm not here—"

Right then, I see it—a flash of silver from Sherry's purse.

The big leather sack is sprawled over the bar like a deer that's been hit and thrown off the highway. Inside, I can see the Shine's leash.

Something comes loose in me.

"Goddamn it, Sherry!" I exclaim. "What'd you do with him?!"

"Fuck you!" she replies, on instinct. "Don't holler at me—"

"Well, where is he?!"

"I don't know! Who?!"

"What's this?" I ask, snatching the leash out of her purse.

"I found it on the sidewalk, you—you . . . *asshole*!"

Mallory is already around the bar. She's skinny as a praying mantis and her grip is strong when she wants it to be. Right now her fingers are closed around my elbow.

"All right Joe," she's saying.

I pull against her, halfhearted.

Seeing me dragged out throws some more coal onto

Sherry's fire, and she gets up, eyes wide, chin dipping as she really winds up for a fastball.

"And you're *lousy* in bed—," she hollers, freezing as she hears herself. A ripple passes through all the shoulders of the people hunched over the bar.

Well, shit. Now I'm in for it.

The Goose is my place, you see? I can't imagine leaving here. But I got a feeling Mr. Nice Guy won't be so nice once he hears about this. They say you don't shit where you eat and all, and I knew better on that account, too.

What a fucking day I've got going here.

"Thanks, Sher," I mutter, as Mallory shoves me out the door and onto the sidewalk where I belong. I automatically collapse into my usual rickety chair, the leash clenched in my hands. Mallory turns around and kicks the stop on the front door and yanks the window closed to cut us off from the dark grotto inside the Goose. She stands there staring at me.

"Should I push off, Mal?" I ask her.

Mallory's steel pincers are settled on her hips and her wide watery blue eyes are set on me. Her reddish-blond eyebrows are raised high over a starscape of freckles, and I realize she looks worried. Which surprises me.

"I don't know," she says. "Are you okay?"

The Shine is helpless and stolen and he was counting on me. My only friend—the only one who can stand being near me for more than five minutes—is a goddamn robot. And I still can't hold up my end of the bargain.

Okay isn't the word.

"Dave is looking for you," she adds. "He sounded pissed off."

In moments of panic, they say sometimes a person goes on autopilot.

"Another round, hey, Mallory?" I ask.

I try not to sound pathetic saying it, but that's just not possible.

Joe learns important information.

So the Shine is disappeared—possibly thanks to a vindictive harpy with spiderwebs tattooed all over her neck—and I've got no idea how to get him back. I'm going to lose my job and my best friend and maybe even my favorite roost here at the Goose.

A lot of stink eye is coming out of that window.

I sit and turn the leash over in my hands some more, but there's no clue there. So I take to looking for the answer at the bottom of my shot glass. Not there either.

At any given moment I can only think of a couple things to do and I just finished drinking one of them. So, I set a few bucks under a half-empty beer back, hop up on unsteady legs, and get to hoofing it up the block.

Scanning the corner where I left him, I see no trace of the robot. I start to think about asking people if they've seen a goddamn loose robot but then remember I smell like spilled whiskey, and it's Portland and speaking to people here scares the shit out of them. Instead, I pick a direction and start down a side street.

I walk like that until I'm sweaty, looking for some glimpse of my pal.

But the Shine doesn't leave tracks and he isn't loud and he's become a common enough sight that people probably won't call the cops on him. Shining Armor sure as shit could have wandered, but more likely Adrian sold him to some two-bit junky and my best friend is in a pickup truck on his way to a pawn shop.

I only hope they don't strip him down for parts.

Just then I notice a mail van chugging up the street. A familiar chubby face is swimming behind its dusty windshield. Turning on my heel, I hook it right up somebody's driveway and keep going until I'm hidden behind a narrow Victorian house. Pressing my back against the mossy concrete foundation, I sit still and listen as the van idles past and keeps going.

Fat Dave is out here looking for me. Well, that's it, I suppose I'm up shit's creek. Time to do what I usually do in this situation. I wheel around and head back to the bar.

At the Goose, I see my money is still on the goddamn table along with my half-drunk beer. Mallory sure takes her sweet time. I drop back into my usual seat and allow myself to take a long, hangdog sigh.

Then I notice a shadow slinking toward me and I remember there are a lot of eyes besides mine on this street. And this guy headed my way is a regular panopticon.

Jim—everybody calls him Jimbo—is tough to figure. He walks around in a little shuffle, shoulders hunched like it was cold. His head is pointed down, but his eyes are up. He's watching, but his gaze never lands on you. His fingers are bent to hold a cigarette whether he's got one at the moment or not, and he's got that permanent five o'clock shadow of a lifelong drunk.

Jimbo doesn't stop here at the Goose much—he's the type that coasts up and down the street all day long, back and forth, like the walking dead. Except you know what he does? He picks up trash when he sees it, holds doors for people, things like that. He's a goddamn Good Samaritan, on permanent patrol, and if you start looking out for them you'll find there's a lot of people like that.

"Hey, Jimbo."

I say it the way everybody says it, and he nods, balding head bobbing, and keeps walking past like he does with everybody.

"You got a second?" I ask, gesturing to my table.

Jimbo kind of coasts to a stop, not looking at me, just waiting in the same kind of way that the Shine waits when I ask him to. He's got that curl in his spine like you see on a whipped dog. There's a story there, I'll bet. But I don't really want to know it.

"You seen anything weird last couple of days?"

He shrugs and starts ambling off. Too vague. I gotta tighten it up.

"You see who did it? Who took the Shine?"

Jimbo stops. He nods at the empty chair. I nod back, so he sits.

"Mal!" I call into the Goose. "Another round when you get a chance, please?"

Sitting hunched, Jimbo's gnarled fingers find each other, tying themselves into a knot over the table, like he's praying. And he probably is—praying for what Mallory's bringing.

"You saw him?" I ask. "Was it a lady with neck tattoos? A guy with a guitar?"

Jimbo turns his head to the side. It wasn't either of those people. But Jimbo also isn't giving up names, not without getting the juice first. Problem is that Mallory will take twenty minutes to make it out here, slogging through all the horse crap that Hemingway and the rest are throwing at her by way of scintillating conversation.

The thing with Mallory is this—it's not that she isn't terrible at her job. She is. But as a customer, you've got to have perspective. She considers those old buzzards at the bar to be her adopted grandparents. When Johnny Morals passed away last winter she leaked tears behind the bar for a week. And he left her his car. So you know the buzzards feel the same way about her.

I go ahead and nudge my half-full beer back across the table to Jimbo. He decides to take it and I let out the breath I was holding.

"I didn't see," he says, wiping beer off his upper lip.

"Damn."

He shrugs. I sigh. I got a feeling, though.

"But?" I ask.

"The robot," he says, pronouncing it "ro-butt."

"Yeah?"

"It's got cameras on it. Records things."

"Yeah, but the Shine's gone—"

He's waving his hand at me, shaking his head.

"Things that could be used as evidence. By the cops."

This guy isn't slow. His brain is moving fast. Lot faster than mine.

"The Shine saw them bridge kids robbing the pigs," I say.

Jimbo nods. Leaning on an elbow, I look over his shoulder and spot Sherry sitting inside the Goose. She's glaring at me through the sliding window with a look so malignant it would make cancer pack up and hit the road. The pint glass held to her lips is filled with ice and vodka and hate.

"Thanks, Jimbo," I say, slapping the table. "I owe you one, buddy."

Joe picks a fight.

Everything goes down under the I-5 highway that runs like a spine through the middle of the west side of Portland. It's an elevated highway, snaking close to the ground until it leaps up and turns into the Fremont Bridge—like a colossus that stepped out of some kid's dinosaur book, only bigger.

Underneath, you've got to deal with the constant thunder of traffic passing by twenty stories overhead, but you got no rain. Depending on the state of things, by the whim of whatever mayor or police chief we have, it's either a thriving tent city or a barren wasteland.

Right now it's trending toward the former.

I start noticing the trash on the street a few blocks before I get there, and my hands tighten on the leash like it was a weapon. Which it could be, I guess. Around here you can see scorch marks on the pavement from old barrel fires, and tarps tucked against leaning chain-link fences, the bones of cardboard poking through underneath.

There's a whole complicated ecosystem at work in a place like this, but the one constant is the grind of age. The young ones are always the most dangerous ones, and that goes for anywhere you find yourself.

The urchins are already milling around me on bicycles, doing lazy circles, most with their faces covered in bandanas. Lot of dogs are wandering around, belonging to anybody and nobody. There are a lot of observations to make here, and a whole lot of shit waiting to go down.

I just keep my legs moving, pushing quickly through the homeless camp as it gets thicker under the shadow of the bridge. My head is on the swivel, looking for the Shine or whatever might be left of the poor sap.

That pile of tarps, I'm thinking. *That's where they've got him.*

Planting a heel in the mud I pivot and head straight toward a pile of dirt-streaked rain tarps with blocky shapes under them. Before I get ten steps, a hand closes over my bicep and a kid in a black hoodie is pulling me back.

"Where you going, mister?" he's asking, eyes dark over a bandana.

"Taking back what's mine," I say, yanking my arm back.

He swipes for me but I'm already hoofing it, like an asshole, like a dope who thinks he's invincible. Friendship will make you do these things.

I almost make it to the tarps before the urchin tackles me. The kid knocks me onto my knees in the mud, and I catch myself with skinned palms. Then he stands up and starts kicking me in the ribs and back. Meanwhile, I'm crawling toward the tarps.

"Shine!" I'm shouting, closing my fingers over the edge of the tarp. I drag it away to reveal a glittering pile of metal—a tangle of half-stripped bicycles, stinking of spray paint and grease. It's only a bunch of stolen bikes.

The Shine isn't here.

Just then, the kid gets me by the scruff of the neck and drags me back. Heels cutting furrows into the mud, I'm just trying to get on my feet.

"Shine," says the kid. "That's a stupid name for a bike."

"Hey!" calls somebody. "Leave him alone! What's the matter with you, dude? He's an old man!"

"That's right!" I'm agreeing, because I've got no shame where the composition of my ribs are concerned. Getting your head kicked in is a young man's game, and they can keep it. "I'm defenseless, for chrissake."

The kid drops me and I manage to get up, smears of mud caked over my pants.

"And I'm muddy, too, now, thanks to you, you goddamn urchin—"

Now I see who the voice of my savior belongs to—it's Adrian the busker, that criminal. *How is he calling me old,* I'm thinking. *He's nearly my age.*

"Adrian," I sputter. "You son of a bitch. What'd you do with him—"

"Nothing, nothing." He's waving at me, trying to reassure me. I'm rolling up the sleeves of my flannel shirt, hot again. Ready to wave my fists around.

"It's Sherry," he says, palms up. "It's the girl I'm after, you dope."

"Sherry?" I ask. "What do you want with her?"

"I'm in love with her."

Oh Jesus Christ.

"Oh Jesus Christ," I say. "Get out of here with that . . . malarkey."

"Me and Sherry have been hooking up for a while now, Joe. So I sent the Shine off up the street and left his leash where she'd find it. I knew you'd freak the fuck out."

"You set me up? Goddamn it, Adrian. Of all the cockamamie—"

"Sherry's too good for a degenerate like you."

He says it with a straight face.

"Me?!" I sputter. "You—you sleep in the *park* for chrissake!"

"I love her, Joe. Do you?"

Just over Adrian's shoulder, I see Mr. Nice Guy walking quick across the trash-strewn field, mouth pinched in anger. Sherry's husband has his fists clenched tight, knuckles white. He must have heard about what she said in the bar today. Even with his hair parted like a little boy, I can tell he's out for my blood.

"Oh great," I mutter. "This guy."

"I'm being serious," says Adrian, not noticing the new arrival.

"It's a misunderstanding!" I shout to Mr. Nice Guy, ignoring Adrian and his ridiculous proclamations of love.

Now, Mr. Nice Guy breaks into a run, a roar building in his throat.

"Now wait just a goddamn second!" I shout, hands up, backpedaling as the spurned husband lumbers toward me and Adrian.

"What're you—," asks Adrian, finally starting to turn around.

And that's when Mr. Nice Guy cracks my least favorite busker up against the side of the head. The old guy still wears that harmless green fleece jacket like he was about to pick his grandkids up from school, but he's also hollering at the top of his lungs. Adrian goes down in a tumble of coats, gray-brown hair flying.

"Fight!" shouts the urchin kid.

I'd almost forgot about him, but my ribs are still lost in memory about those boots of his. Mr. Nice Guy is pistoning his fist into Adrian's messy mass of coats and scarves.

And meanwhile, an army of whackos and criminals from under the bridge is streaming toward us, rubbernecking and cheering on this pathetic battle that's unfolding.

"Hey," I'm shouting. "Calm down, buddy!"

Fist raised, Mr. Nice Guy looks up at me.

"He's been sleeping with my wife!" he says through clenched teeth.

I take a few steps back.

"Oh," I say. "Well then."

Adrian is laid out on his back, trying to fend off Sherry's husband and shouting for help. Just then the overexcited urchin tackles them both. And more of the kids are crowding around, some of them joining the fight. Most of them are going after Mr. Nice Guy, but not all of them. For his part, Mr. Nice Guy is giving them back some hell of his own and good for him.

I guess he wasn't really that nice, after all.

With careful steps, I start backing away from the mob. I've got no dog in this fight anymore, so I'm ready to ghost the whole situation.

"Joe!" shouts somebody, as I move away from the scrum.

Oh, for chrissake. What now?

And there's my boss Dave, puttering across the muddy lot in his beat-up post office van, leaning out the open door and shouting my name. He must have tracked me down from the Goose, and come looking for the Shine.

I wave him off, pretend I don't know him. I got nothing for him.

"Joe!"

I notice three or four bridge kids zeroing in on the van.

They start pelting the vehicle with bicycle parts and mud clods, laughing and giving chase. Dave leans back inside the van, in a panic now, clinging to the steering wheel and frantically trying to slide the door closed.

I keep walking.

Bandanas and army boots, streaming past me. Shouting and punching and tackling, weals of muddy dirt torn by steel-toed boots.

An engine revs up and Dave's mail van lurches past me, out of control, a couple urchins hanging off the side of it. He pops a curb at about walking speed and the whole she-bang crunches into a bridge pillar.

Another step and this time I keep going without looking back.

Next thing I know, I'm back at the Goose.

Joe is reunited with the Shine.

"Shine?" I ask. "Shine!"

The little walker is standing there next to my usual seat, looking lost and worse for the wear. He's like a cat that's been out all night, nonchalant, but with dirt caked around his feet and crumbling leaves pasted to his back.

"You villain," I exclaim, coming up on him. "Where the hell you been?"

I put a hand on his shoulder and turn him around half a step. I try to check the battery readout on the side of his head but it's muddy. I spit on my thumb and rub off the dirt and see he's on virtually zero power.

"Damn, you barely made it back," I say. "Let's get you some juice. Can you walk?"

In response, the Shine takes a trudging step.

"All right—"

"Joe! Damnit, Joe!"

And there's Dave, his dented-up mail van idling on the curb. He's wrapped in a green sweater, with a whole lot of sweat on his forehead. He looks like a Christmas tree dragging himself out of the van and struggling up the sidewalk, waving a hand to get my attention.

"Hello, Dave," I say.

"What," he pants, "what's the deal? What were you doing today? There's a big fight down the street, it's crazy—"

I put a hand on the Shine's shoulder. Snap his leash into its spot.

"Don't know anything about it."

But Dave has caught up now and he's starting to get his breath, God help me.

"Don't give me that," he says. "What were you doing down there? Why wasn't your unit with you?"

Ah, fuck it. I put my hands out.

"To tell you the truth, Dave, the Shine got away from me a little bit today."

"I know. I check your logs."

I blink.

"My logs?"

"Yeah, the unit keeps track of its path. You didn't think we'd just let it loose without any way to track it? With *you*?"

Now this is a surprise.

"My *logs*?!" I repeat, like an idiot.

"You're doing the work of ten men, Joe. The paths you take through the city. You two really get around—"

"So you've been spying on us? You knew where the Shine was today?!"

"Why, sure. It looked like an odd route. Wandering—"

"Damn it, Dave, that's an invasion—"

I've got too much anger to express, and it just comes out in a single word.

"Why . . . why, you goddamn *tomato*."

I really let him have it. Now I'm embarrassed. Just like that.

"Tomato?" asks Dave.

"It's the shirt you were wearing. The day I met you—"

"I been called a lot of things, but a tomato? It doesn't make any sense, Joe."

"That's what I'm trying to tell you—"

"It's not even an insult."

"Just shut up, will you? Stop interrupting—"

"Matter of fact, I *like* tomatoes," he says, drawing up his double chin in a little pout.

It's too much for me. I shouldn't—he's my boss, after all—but I shout.

"Good!"

Now it's his turn to blink, and finally shut up for a second.

"*Good,* you goddamn tomato. I'm glad you like vegetables. Now, will you leave me alone and let me take the Shine back to his office? I got work to do."

Dave shakes his head at me, trying to contain a little smile.

"You weren't worried about him, were you?" he asks.

I snort.

"Okay," he says. "I'll see you tomorrow, Joe."

"Yeah," I mutter, walking away, leading the Shine behind me. "Okay, Dave."

"Take it easy, Joe," he calls after me.

"Yeah."

Goddamn tomato.

As soon as we round the corner, I turn to the Shine.

"Stop for a second?" I ask and he pauses. "Are you thinking what I'm thinking?"

With a rap, I knock on his compartment and it flies open. A flask of Jameson pops out into my hand like magic. Unscrewing it, I take a deep breath of warm summer air and break out into a little smile. My ribs hurt, but not that much, all things considered.

"Hell, Shine," I say to him, "it's still a pretty good day for a walk."

Joe and the Shine go for a walk.

ONE

FOR

SORROW

A CLOCKWORK DYNASTY STORY

PART I

The dark woods; a lost boy with the fey sight; and an inauspicious meeting.

Alas, alas, how terrible to have wisdom, when it brings no profit to him that is wise! This I knew well, but had forgotten it; else I would not have come here.

—Sophocles, *Oedipus Rex*

England, 1756

The fall of raindrops in the empty countryside forms a pattern that has become a familiar comfort. Twitching leaves and rippling puddles. English oaks sway, rough bark stained with water, roots worming through heaving clumps of sweetgrass. The woods seem alive with the traces of ghosts playing in the dusk.

I stand here during the hours that men walk.

A soaked and tattered lace dress hangs from my thin wooden bones. I can feel stripes of my long black hair clinging to the handcrafted planes of my face. In these times, I do not bother blinking or breathing.

I imagine myself as a scarecrow, waiting.

And yet a scarecrow is endowed with such clear and simple intent. I can only envy that, for my own purpose is more elusive. I am *avtomat,* and my makers left a single Word written upon my heart—a compulsion that I have followed into an abyss.

My Word is *logicka.*

Obeying the dictates of logic has sent me roaming these marshy woods on bare porcelain feet. The cold does not send shivers through my body. Though I appear to be a girl of twelve, this appearance has grown superficial. My breath is silent and my limbs still, save for a slight, shuddering clockwork pulse that forms another pattern, equally steady as the rain. But in these patterns I have found no meaning.

I am months into my wandering when the human boy sees me.

Rough-featured and about fourteen, he has freckled cheeks and ha'penny-blond hair. He does not cry out when his wide green eyes find my figure where I stand knee-deep in the marsh, my features shrouded by lolling tongues of grass. Instead of running away, he pushes toward me through mud and branches.

He comes nearer and I do not move.

These wild woods have gnawed at me. Brambles and branches have torn and scratched my dress and stockings. The calf-skin leather of my face, once smooth with ash and cream, is dark and damp now with the glint of brasswork beneath. I have become a monster—alive and not alive. The boy's eyes widen in wonder and horror.

But he does not flee.

"Georgie!" comes a shout. It's a grown man, somewhere beyond the wall of reeds. I can hear him splashing and cursing. "Where've you got to?!"

The boy's mouth opens.

I lift a porcelain finger to my lips. *Shh.* If necessary, I will pull him into these woods and ensure he never emerges again. We *avtomat* must protect the secret of our existence, always, and even from the innocent.

Georgie exhales, leaning closer.

"Who are you?" he asks.

I turn and walk deeper into the marshy woods, not sparing him another glance. There is no satisfactory answer to his question, nor any reason to respond. And yet, I find myself taking care to move slow enough for the boy to follow.

In this prehistoric domain, every tree and rock is a constant reminder that inanimate things still live. Logs fallen centuries ago are covered in life—sprouting a writhing mass of plants, vines, and moss. Curled brown leaves blanket the marsh and buds of green blossom, swaying and fluttering under the talons of tiny birds. All of it is falling apart, decaying, but also growing up, clawing and pushing—alive.

If my clockwork failed and I fell to the forest floor, limbs frozen, I wonder if I would know the quiet pleasure of becoming part of this eternal cycle. Lying still under the creeping moss, would I come to understand the colossal patterns that grow roots in millennia? Or will I always live in this series of eye-blink moments?

I continue to walk, wisps of my torn white dress tracing the water's surface. The boy called Georgie follows. I know he has already seen too much.

This boy. His master. They do not belong here.

During my sojourn, I have witnessed a kind of beautiful *logicka* nestled in wild places like this. Every forgotten stream chooses its meandering path according to rules older than humankind. I have urged my thoughts to wander the same paths.

It is men who take the lovely natural patterns of the wood and smear them into hard corners and straight lines and flat spaces. I have grown to hate the sight of a redbrick chimney looming through tree branches. The erect spine of a steeple feels so simple and primitive compared to the great chattering canopy of a millennia-old oak, alive and ancient, wind sifting through its many outstretched arms.

I despise the humans, and yet I am evidence of their craft.

A lost mastery over nature has manifested itself in my form—the form of *avtomat*. Long ago, a race of man took the tools of the wilderness—dirt, clay, metal, bone, and wood—and twisted them into a simulacrum of themselves. My hatred smolders, but it can never fully ignite with the knowledge that the ones I despise made me.

And I was made to serve them.

I stop in the center of a damp meadow, surrounded by narrow ranks of pine trees that seem to judge. Turning, I wait for the boy to emerge. By now he is muddy and scared, a tentative vision of golden light splitting shadowed trunks.

Sitting on a canted log, heels dangling, I wait for him.

"Hello?" he calls, approaching slowly.

I turn my head to look at the blond boy, my torn face empty and placid. He is quite beautiful. It will be a shame to kill him.

"Are you well?" he asks. "What's happened to your face?"

Remembering to breathe, I fill my lungs and speak for the first time in several years. My voice feels as though it belongs to someone else, from some other time, as a complicated mechanism still performs its work in my breast.

"I am Elena," I say. "My face is this way because I am not of your race. And because I am very old."

Surprisingly, he accepts this without question.

"You're of the honest folk, ain't you? The fey folk of the wood? My ma used to speak of your kind."

All strange things are cloaked in myth, eventually.

"Are you a queen?" he asks.

I nod.

"Where's your kingdom?"

"It is fallen. Once, I studied by candlelight in stone halls buried within barrow hills. I danced in golden palaces. But the others of my kind have left in search of their own purpose, and now I am alone."

I look in the direction of the rough voice I heard earlier.

"And what of your family, boy?"

He pauses.

"My master and I are traveling through. Looking for work."

"Truth rings like a silver bell," I respond. "And lies fester."

The boy and his master are not in these godforsaken wastes looking for work. Not when an abandoned mansion full of forgotten treasure rises from the marshes less than a mile from here.

He blushes and looks away.

A few have tried, but the remote location and the mansion's reputation for being haunted have kept thieves at bay. And those who came too close to my deserted home have found me waiting for them in the countryside.

I hear shouting beyond the meadow. *Georgie!*

"You and your master shouldn't have come here," I say, bowing my head. The torn skin of my face crumples into a frown as I gather my resolve. As I stand up from my perch on the log, the boy's tanned face goes pale.

"Does . . . does it hurt?" he asks, his breath whispering over dry lips.

I blink, surprised by the question. It is his own life he should worry for, not mine. Reaching up, I run fingers lightly over my jawline.

"Nothing here can hurt me," I say.

I'm closer to the boy now. He is a bit taller than me, gangly and lean. His limbs are strong, but I can see ribs rippling under his rough canvas shirt. His teeth are white and eyes sharp, and a stipple of bruises ride the ridge of his neck.

Georgie?! You bloody bastard!

This master of his bears more inspection.

"And you?" I ask.

"What d'you mean?"

"Do you suffer, Georgie?"

He smiles weakly, backing away.

"I'm alive, aren't I?"

PART II

A cruel master; the suffering of youth; and an offer of assistance.

Life is an unfoldment. To understand the things at our door is the best preparation for understanding those that lie beyond.

—Hypatia of Alexandria (AD 350)

Watching him retreat from the flooded meadow, knees flinging mud, I decide I like this rough boy—even if he is too young to know anything and will likely never live long enough to learn.

This affection is an unfamiliar feeling. Rare.

Too many human beings have come and gone, too rapidly. But I sense something calm and still in this youth. He does not seem to know fear.

Georgie reminds me of my brother.

Peter and I fled to London sixty years ago. Before that, we watched generations rise and fall on the moonlit streets of Moscow. Across countries and time, we saw modes of dress and languages melt through infinite configurations. But the people always remained the same. Made of flesh and bound to it, all folk obey routines of food and worship and family. Praying to their gods, they despise themselves for their weaknesses while at the same time claiming the rest of the world as their own.

I took the mansion after my brother abandoned me to fight the war in India. For a time, I entertained myself by holding court with the world's great minds. But I found a dispiriting sameness among them. None could see beyond my childlike form, and their condescension never ceased.

Great men and women, surely, but shortsighted.

Defluat amnis, the time runs on, and I grew tired of humanity. Their faces seemed to ebb and flow, endless waves lapping a dirty beach, each generation inching progress forward like a meandering line of rotting sea foam.

Once I had learned all they could teach, it was logical to

send the faces away from me. And in the crumbling shell of my mansion I rambled alone in dark hallways—the ghost of a child who was never born. One day, I had the urge to walk out the front door. Leaving it open behind me, I continued into the wild gardens and then beyond into the damp wood where the humans believe fey kingdoms lurk.

And now this boy has led me back home.

Georgie and his master are bivouacked near a small stream about a half mile from the mansion. In the misty night, I spy them through vines and mossy tree limbs and my own tangled locks. The boy seems to sense me, glancing nervously into the darkness. His master, a coughing, spitting vulture of a man, senses nothing but his own base needs.

The gaunt middle-aged man must be a leatherworker by trade. He sits beside the fire and scrapes flesh from a stiff horse hide, knuckles caked in rusty blood. He does not speak to the boy except to curse him or give him an order to tend the fire or fetch a tool. Though his master clearly fails him, Georgie watches, alert. I notice the boy's fingers twitching as he imagines moving them in the same practiced patterns as his master.

Lurking around the fire, the master quaffs gin and menaces the boy. It causes me to think of the twin stilettos sheathed at my hips. The talented mechanician who revived me from a fathomless sleep found these ancient weapons already in my possession. They are sized for a child and I use them as naturally as I think.

"Come, it's time," the master says well after dusk, grunting as he rises.

The boy dutifully begins to stuff a haversack with limp canvas bags, tying it with a thick hemp rope. At the same time, he speaks low and quiet.

"Are you quite sure? Perhaps we'd better wait until morning or—"

"That preventive man will be there during the day, watching over the wreck. The one who caused your delay earlier, isn't it? You seen him yourself, or has your memories failed you?"

"Yes, sir, but—"

The old man lunges and slaps Georgie across the face. Then he snatches away the knotted rope and violently lashes the boy. The motions are fast, even for a human, off-balance and filled with anger. The boy is knocked to the ground where he lies writhing, not daring to stand up or cry out.

"But nothing," grunts the master, tossing the rope down. "Obey me and stop working that jaw."

As the man hitches his leg back for a kick, I draw a stiletto. The ring of the oiled blade leaving its metal sheath is unmistakable, even cloaked as I am in darkness. The frogs and crickets of the wood cease their cacophony. The stream trickles silently past my feet in silver ripples.

The master twists his head slowly, bleary eyes wide to the night.

"What's out there?" he asks, standing over the bleeding boy. "Who is it?"

I am a pale statue, unseen in the gloom beyond the ring of feeble light thrown by their peat brick campfire.

"Boy, d'you know who's out there?" he asks in a low voice.

"I don't, master."

The master is silent, nervously picking at his fingers with the scraping knife. Finally, he says, "Load that canvas and don't make me strike you again. We enter that manor at midnight, if we have to face the devil himself."

The boy finishes preparing in silence, and my blade finds its sheath.

Finishing his work, Georgie steps a short distance into the darkness. He stops beside the stream, kneels in the mud, and wipes blood from his forehead with dirty palms. His cheeks are streaked with tears. The raised welts of the beating stripe his forearms and neck.

"Why do you allow it?" I ask, from the shadows. "You are stronger."

Georgie hesitates, then continues washing his face.

"My master makes decisions. I live with them."

"You are trapped under a yoke."

"A yoke is the chance to do good work, ma'am," he responds, shivering.

The boy has been beaten and neglected, his education ignored, dragged through this world over rough cobblestones. Yet his spirit thrives. I wonder what unique quality of mind, what blindness, allows him to survive? It is a strange variety of armor that this boy wears—and I have no weapon to break it.

"What made you this way, Georgie?" I ask.

He shrugs, standing up and wrapping arms around himself. His skin is smooth and pale, a dark crescent of blood gleaming over his eyebrow.

"What else is there?" he asks. "What else can you do?"

"Leave," I say. "Go out on your own."

"My fees are paid up. It's a seven-year term."

"You could walk away."

"I'd lose my apprenticeship," he says. "I'd lose my trade."

"Everything will be lost eventually. All things are moving away from us. Why not let them go?"

"Pardon me, m'lady, but I suppose I'm only good at hanging on," he says, eyes wide and unseeing in the darkness, his teeth shining as he smiles to himself. "Perhaps I'm ignorant, but it's all I've ever known to do."

"You are not ignorant," I say. "It's all any of us do."

PART III

An old manor house—abandoned, or seemingly so; a pair of criminals; and a realization.

One for sorrow, Two for mirth.
Three for a funeral, Four for birth.
Five for heaven, Six for hell.
Seven for the devil, his own self.

—Nursery rhyme, 1700s

The abandoned mansion looms out of the night, windows dark, roofline cutting through silvery sheets of light rain. As I walk nearer, I see the accumulated damage of long neglect. I sent the servants away all at once on a fall afternoon. The doors and windows still hang open like skeletal, broken jaws.

Crates have been delivered in my absence, dumped along the front path. They must have been sent by my brother from distant places, artifacts and treasures looted during his long time at war in India. Only the solitude and secrecy of this place have allowed them to remain unmolested. Ahead, the sculpted figure of a water nymph emerges from a mossy fountain, feet lost in black water and decayed leaves. Her lips are rough stone, pursed as if she is about to shout a warning.

Hushed voices resonate under the hiss of raindrops.

Seating myself beside the fountain, I allow my body to become still in the way of stone—just another inanimate facet of this estate, like the carved gargoyles perched among shuffling crows along the sagging roofline.

Soon, two foolish men come creeping through the night.

The bigger one is drunk and unsteady on skinny legs, a vicious-looking knife clenched in one hand. And the other is my Georgie, hunched over with a haversack and a heavy pry bar.

". . . four, five, six . . . *seven*," whispers the boy.

"What're you muttering about?" asks his master.

"Counting the ravens, sir," he says, pointing up at the roof.

Seven dark-feathered shapes dot the gutters, black feathers waxy under the light of a full moon. "One for sorrow, two for mirth—"

"Bah!" interrupts the master. "Nursery rhymes. There are no bloody omens in the flight of birds."

"Yes, sir."

"Hand me the bar," says the man, striding past me and mounting the front steps. The door is halfway open, bloated with rain and stuck.

"Sir," says Georgie, complying. "I fear we're attracting an awful evil gaze, coming here like this."

"What's abandoned is ours to take," responds the man. "And this wreck is occupied by nothing but spiders and mice."

"I . . . I—," stutters Georgie, eyes landing on me where I sit beside the fountain.

"What?" hisses the master.

Finger to my lips, I stand and walk away silently.

Allowing the men to continue, I enter the mansion through the pantry door. My bare feet tap over rain-swollen wood as I explore familiar halls. Distantly, I hear the boy and his master as they stumble through the cold darkness.

There is only one room that matters to me in this mansion—the parlor.

It is the room in which I once wrote letters and took my correspondence. The room in which I first delved beneath the layers of my own artificial flesh. The piles of notes and half-finished experiments carry the secret of my true existence.

I wait in the hallway outside the parlor door, listening patiently as the two intruders ramble through empty corridors. Occasionally, I hear a clink or rattle as items are placed in the canvas sacks. It does not move me, to be robbed. Objects no longer have any meaning. Only the knowledge matters.

Besides, Georgie doesn't know any better. I would be doing him a favor to remove his master from the world. And I could allow the boy to survive it, with his assumptions of my fey ancestry. Ultimately, it is to my advantage to let him spread rumor of a fey queen protecting this cursed manor and its wild gardens. The superstition of the people is strong, and it guides their behavior with more power than the rule of law.

Through the window behind me, a great moon pushes her face through a haze of clouds. Her gentle light lands on my shoulders, illuminating my small silhouette.

A flicker of candlelight curls up the stairwell, batting shadows through clinging cobwebs. The man hacks and coughs, kicking leaves around the sweeping wooden staircase. Georgie's voice is low and insistent, begging his master to stop.

The master's head appears at the top of the stairs, dark eyes glittering. He inspects the great hall and its paintings and gilded cornices. Again, I am unnoticed.

But the boy sees me.

"Oh no," he moans. "Master, please, we must retreat now."

The man peers into the moonlight, shading his eyes and taking a tentative step forward.

"What . . . what is that?" he asks. "Is it a doll?"

"*Please,* master . . ."

He moves closer, not understanding.

"What is that thing?" he asks.

Georgie tugs on his master's arm, digging in his heels. The man turns and shoves him to the floor, the heavy canvas sack dragging him down. Shrugging off the straps, the boy crawls, supplicating himself, begging and pulling at the man's heels.

Stopping before me, the master leans closer. He reaches out a shaking fingertip and touches the cool mask of my face.

I step back and draw my stiletto.

The master shudders and flinches in terror, his chin dipping and knees shivering with adrenaline. I reach up and wrap porcelain fingers around his throat, pulling his terror-stricken face to mine. His cheeks twitch with fright, chest heaving as he prepares to give voice to a scream.

"You should have listened to your boy," I say.

He tries to scream now and I pinch my fingers closed.

Nothing comes out but a choked grunt. I feel his sagging chest dimple under the point of my blade. And I prepare to thrust.

"No!" shouts Georgie. "No, m'lady. Please!"

The boy throws himself between us, hand falling over my fist. He will become a strong man one day, but today I am stronger. My blade remains poised firmly against his master's chest.

"He abuses you," I say. "I will end him."

Georgie whispers urgently.

"I am bound to my master and I must serve. If I find he is weak, then I must make him strong—"

"He doesn't care about you. He will use you."

"He gives me a purpose. I can't run from that."

How long have I been running, lost in the woods?

Stiletto glinting, I ponder these words. I assumed humanity had nothing left to teach me, but the boy speaks wisdom. He commands not facts or figures or lost tongues, but a simple virtue of character—a perspective through which I can see the world with fresh eyes and make fresh conclusions.

"M'lady," he whispers. "Please. You're terrible strong, but please—don't use your power to harm us."

I was made in the image of a fallen race and bound to their inferior ancestors. *Logicka* told me to find knowledge elsewhere. But what if the answer is not to walk away from them? What if I must lift them up to their previous glory?

On his knees, the master moans, his hands clasped together now in prayer, shaking. Eyes squeezed closed, he is crying and praying in the darkness. Pressing harder with the tip of my blade, I whisper into the master's ear.

"Do better, sir."

With a nod to the boy, I sheathe my blade and depart.

Minutes later, I watch two silhouettes emerge from the decaying mansion. One moves slowly on birdlike legs, aged a hundred years in a night, gibbering in mortal fear and horror. The other is confident, an arm around his master's shoulders.

Georgie drops the pry bar on the porch, along with the canvas sacks and any pretense of robbing the mansion. Both of them are survivors now, no longer prowlers. They depart with something far more precious than treasure—their own lives.

"It's fine, sir," whispers the boy. "You'll be fine."

The man staggers, moaning about the devil.

"It was only a vision, master. It weren't Lucifer."

The man stops, holds the boy's shoulders.

"Do you think so, Georgie? But I seen it. The devil spoke to us!"

"A warning, sir. To put us on another path."

Nodding vigorously, the man emits a short, hysterical laugh.

"Yes, yes, Georgie. I believe it's truth! Truth, you speak. I should have listened. You—you're a wise boy, for your years. It was a gift we been given. A specter sent to counsel us. We been set on the right path now."

"That's right, sir."

"I've treated you terribly," says the master, his voice muted by the mist and earth and water. "Terribly. But we'll set things right . . ."

I follow them back into the woods, finding the call of

primal forces no longer pulls quite so ferociously at me. The eternal cycles of this wood follow *logicka,* but it is an endless, pixie-led loop that goes nowhere.

These trees will grow, but they will never remember.

I think of the talented souls I communicated with so long ago. Those men and women had nothing left to teach me, but with a little guidance I could help them accomplish so much more. Their entire race could be molded, pulled into a better future, a place where the exquisite potential of their minds could be expressed in shining cities of gold—a place where the children of their intellects can thrive in peace.

And who better to start with?

In the dawn, I find the boy watering his horses and preparing for the journey home. His master is laid up against a tree, sleeping as if comatose.

"Georgie," I say, quietly. "You are a noble boy."

Pausing with one hand on the horse's bridle, his eyes find my face where it is shaded among branches and wet leaves. The dew crowns each leaf with sparkling glory in the morning sunlight.

It is a glory that will evaporate today, and return tomorrow.

"Our races have much to learn from each other. I had forgotten that, and you reminded me. Thank you."

"Thank you, m'lady," he says. "For your mercy."

Trying to hide his fright, the boy throws a saddlebag onto the back of the horse. Tightens the strap and yanks on it to test it.

"What is your surname?" I ask.

He turns, and in his silhouette I can see the man he'll become.

"I'm Timms, m'lady."

"Georgie Timms. In time, you may convince yourself that I never existed. That I was a figment or a dream. But one day I will find you again."

"M'lady—"

I raise a finger to my lips. *Shh.*

"See that you do not forget me, Mr. Timms. For I do not plan to forget you."

SPECIAL AUTOMATIC

The boy was small for seventeen, on the verge of adulthood and unaware of it. He stank of stale sweat, hunched over a soldering iron at a desk in a sweltering bedroom. Nobody had ever told him to put on deodorant. Nobody had ever told him much.

James often forgot to blink. He had a medical device called a neurostimulator sunk into his brain like a spider-web of metal, its batteries housed in a flesh-colored lump of plastic tucked behind his right ear. Anticipating his brain's rhythms, the implant prevented the metallic haze of a seizure from descending over him. Most of the time it worked.

Brain of a fucking goldfish, according to his older brother Mike.

That assessment wasn't hard for most people to believe, as they let their eyes slide past the slope-shouldered young man, embarrassed by his incongruously large head, stamped as it was with a wide, expressionless face. His features were heroic in proportion, Homeric even, but his bottom lip was disfigured, a lobe of flesh that bobbed whenever he spoke, usually in whispers to himself as his colossal mind wandered its own strange labyrinths.

Nobody had ever told him much, but James had learned plenty.

The walls of his stifling bedroom were lined with stacks of stolen library books. Many of them were mold-eaten or bloated from being left in the rain, but the boy's still face had sat a long time before each one, letting knowledge filter up like radiation into the machinery of his intellect.

Sensing, but not knowing for sure and perhaps not caring, James felt he was somehow invisible to the world, damaged and left behind. In the darkness of utter disregard and neglect, unseen by his brother, his teachers, or the rough boys selling drugs on the corner, James toiled under the bright spotlight of his own focus, relentlessly channeling the information he absorbed from his stacks of moldering books into the oily screen of a scavenged laptop computer.

Abandoned to his own thoughts for almost a decade, James had finally built something incredible and necessary.

The mechanical contraption hung above him, attached to the wall in the spread-arm posture of crucifixion.

It was an unborn creature—dark and calm and terrible.

A box fan rattled from its perch on a splintered windowsill. Outside, waves of scorching sunlight fell against baking asphalt and glinting chain link, lancing up into the bedroom's fluttering roll-down shades and dying there in a muddy yellow haze.

As James worked, spine curved into a question mark, he kept one ear cocked to the street downstairs. His brother would be home from work soon. The anticipation made James both afraid and eager to have it over with. With luck, what passed for Mike's job—collecting drug money—would have gone well and he would already be drunk. Once Mike was asleep, James could sneak down the hall to make a baloney sandwich and drink a glass of water.

After one last dab of liquid metal, James pushed the hot finger of the soldering iron into its cradle and switched it off. His dark empty eyes traced the rivers of metal that coursed over home-pressed circuit boards, double-checking each connection. Then he lifted his face to the machine he had built.

Special Automatic.

The humanoid form hung from a hook James had mounted to the wall. It was much taller than he was, its long, slender limbs crafted from parts James had found on the street or in dumpsters. There were the heavy-duty public street cleaners, and of course the ubiquitous government mail-delivery walkers, and sometimes advertising machines that stumbled into the neighborhood, lost. They were constantly getting bashed to pieces, shoved into the gutters, or dragged behind cars by the neighborhood boys.

When their fun was over, James would emerge, scuttling from piece to piece, considering each bit of metal or plastic before dropping it into a trash bag straining over his shoulder. The machine had come together in Frankensteinian fashion, the pieces coalescing undisturbed in this moldy, forgotten bedroom. And now, it had finally manifested itself, great head hanging, face pointed at the floor, massive shoulders hunched, and long arms spread wide.

James took a deep breath, his maimed lip fluttering. He held it as he switched on the machine. Power surged into its sinewy plastic limbs. A dim light began to smolder in its eyes. And for the first time he could remember, James found that he was not invisible.

A loud humming swelled in his ears, and James felt the warm surge of electrical interference in the threads of metal that coursed through his brain. He closed his eyes as the hint of a seizure skated over him, sucking air through kidney-shaped nostrils.

The deep brain stimulator had been in his head since childhood, poised to deliver a steadying heartbeat to the fetal curl of gray meat whenever it sensed chaos rising up from confused neurons. At night, trying to fall asleep, James sometimes traced his fingers over the battery pack that bulged out behind his ear, feeling that liminal spot where the wire disappeared under his skin.

The battery in the implant had not been refreshed since

before James's mother left him with Mike, and he wasn't sure his brother even remembered it was there. But James was not too worried. With simple tools, he had been able to modify the implant. Now it could report its status. After querying the battery level, the boy knew the device had enough power to last for years.

James opened his eyes, his mind calm again.

Slowly, he raised his arm. Across from him, the dark figure responded by raising its arm, too. And under the rushing thrum of the box fan, the machine and boy saluted each other the same way the boy had seen soldiers do in online cartoons.

The diagnostic test was a success.

James's maimed lip twitched, just once. It was the boy's way of smiling without smiling, and he was unaware that it was happening. He had learned early on that happiness was not something others could tolerate in him.

"Your name is Special Automatic," he whispered.

"Okay," said the machine. Nothing moved as its voice emanated from a battered speaker, but a glow of yellow LEDs pulsed where its mouth would be.

"What do you see?"

Special Automatic lifted its head slightly.

"I see you, James," it said, and the boy's lip twitched again.

Then the boy and machine flinched as a car door slammed outside.

James tiptoed to the window and peered through the box fan's dust-stained slats.

His brother Mike was laid out on the weedy sidewalk below. A bald man in a suit stood over him, forehead glinting with gems of sweat. Elbows akimbo, the big man swung his leg and feinted a kick.

Mike's girlfriend, Delia, shrieked, writhing in a tight dress, her overly made-up face emoting with theatrical vigor.

"C'mon, Connor," she shouted.

The flurry of halfhearted kicks was enough to send Mike scrambling away on his elbows, whining an apology as the bigger man simply laughed. Delia kept shouting, pleading and cursing, pulling on Mike's arms while her purse hung loose from her forearm, the rest of her jangling accessories—earrings, necklace, sunglasses—orbiting her thin body like rogue moons. The bald man turned and walked away, crossing the empty street with his back to the sidewalk, stopping only to shout a stern warning over his shoulder.

James's brother Mike—they called him "Skinny Mike" in the neighborhood—climbed to his feet, shaking Delia off and wiping blood from his nose with a needle-bitten forearm. A rare .38 special automatic handgun nestled against the crook of his brother's back, tucked into his ill-fitting blue jeans like a lump of coal. The weapon evoked fear in most people, but not Connor. Mike's boss was not afraid of anything, and James had heard him called a "bad motherfucker" more than once.

The bald man gave a final glance back, and Mike's head ducked in autonomic deference, the submissive reaction slaved to a kind of metastasized cowardice.

As Connor got in his car, shaking his head in disgust, James's brother craned his neck upward to look at the apartment. Their eyes met through the slats of the spinning fan, and a snarl of shame and anger crawled across his brother's face.

Moving on a wave of panic, James scrambled to escape the apartment.

"Jimmy! Yo! Where are you at?!"

The shouts echoed up the wooden stairs. From where he was already crouched on the fire escape, James could feel the vibrations in the row house as his brother stomped up the shared steps. Obsessively, the boy submarined his thumbnail through layers of flaking paint on the metal slats, picking away the black skin like a scab, revealing green and red and yellow layers below. Ever since his mother had moved out by the airport, the landing had disintegrated into a leper's back of picked paint from the time James spent waiting for his older brother to tire out, or for the drugs or alcohol to wear off.

"I fucking saw you! You shit. Get back in here *right now.*"

Mike's voice was already faltering, the crest of violence pulled under the surf by Delia's low, feminine murmur of "Don't worry about it, baby. . . ."

Ribs still aching from the last time his brother had come home angry, James felt no desire to respond. Mike considered himself an enforcer and debt collector for the local street gang, mostly fetching brown paper bags of money from the same kids they'd grown up with on the block. But even to James it was clear that nobody else feared him, not in the way they did Connor.

It was only the .38 special that extracted grudging respect.

Whether James feared Mike or not was immaterial, as he depended on his brother for food and shelter. His mother showed up every now and then, but the rest of the time Mike was in charge, cashing a check from the government every month on James's account. In return, Mike allowed his younger brother to haunt the splintered apartment.

James had become generally immune to his brother's fists and temper, but he still felt a pinch when he heard *that word* come from inside. As the syllables rang through the window to the fire escape, they hit James like a pair of thrown scissors.

"Retard," Mike said, and even though he would laugh out loud at the suggestion that he feared his little brother in any way, he still said the word quietly, as if on a dare. Some unconscious part of Mike had noticed the strange, subtle twisting of the boy's features when those syllables left his lips.

Inside, Delia shrieked with grating laughter. "C'mon," she said, faintly. "Forget about it."

James clambered down the rungs of the fire escape and threw himself at the concrete sidewalk. After landing on all fours, scraping his knees and elbows, he stood, sucking in his deformed lip. The back of his neck stung with the shame and confusion of that—that *damned*—word.

Recovering, James began to walk, moving deliberately from the alley out into the main street, eyes downcast, turning that grotesque word over in his mind, wearing it smooth like a piece of sea glass. In reverie, James did not notice the two corner boys who watched him emerge from the alley.

Exchanging a grinning glance, the boys set out to follow him.

James was halfway to the corner bodega when he registered the heavy footsteps behind him. The street was mostly empty. No route out.

"Hey 'tardo," came the familiar call.

The skin-colored bulge of plastic behind James's ear was noticeable from a distance and it marked him as different. It always had.

"Where you going?"

James stopped, digging a few crumpled bills out from his pocket. As he turned, a fist sunk into his stomach, collapsing the air out of his diaphragm and leaving his sunken chest spasming. Over the years he had learned not to fall, no matter what; instead he hunched against the cracked brick wall. He did not allow himself to whimper, but a certain amount of mechanical grunting for air was unavoidable.

Fist shaking, he held out crumpled dollars that he had scrounged from between the wall and his brother's mattress. "Here," he croaked, already turning to hobble away.

"Better," said a grinning older boy. Someone had given him a cursive tattoo of his own name on his neck. It read "Claudell."

But James had let go too soon, and the dollars fell to the ground.

"The fuck?" asked Claudell at this unintentional sign of disrespect.

James felt a shove between his shoulder blades that sent him headfirst into the wall. His teeth clacked together as his face hit. Something warm began to course over his temple, and James knew then that he must run.

"Sorry," James panted, darting away, pressing one palm flat against the small cut on his forehead. The other boys did not hear him over the slap of their feet on the ground and their own laughing and taunting. Behind them all, the wind nudged the crumpled dollar bills across the sidewalk like scuttling crabs.

As he ran, blood wetting his palm, James felt a few sharp pieces of brick pelting his back. He continued around the corner to his row house. And as he stampeded up the shared steps to his own front door, he heard that stinging word again. He sucked his lower lip into his mouth and bit into it hard.

The corner boys followed James up the set of stairs, stomping like cattle, the entire building reverberating.

James shoved into the apartment, dashing past a surprised Mike and Delia where they lounged in the living room, and pushed through the door to his tiny bedroom. He barely registered Special Automatic, looming on the wall, still humming with power.

Diving across the room, James rolled onto his back just

as the two boys kicked open the door. Laughing, they lunged into the hot twilight.

And something dark moved.

With electrical speed, Special Automatic clamped scuffed plastic fingers around Claudell's neck, choking off a laugh. The robotic arm hung in the air, rugged and strong, fingers obscuring the greenish cursive tattoo that wrapped around Claudell's neck.

Legs scrabbling, James pushed himself up against the wall, under the shadow of the machine. Over his own breathing, James could hear the wet, glottal noises of a compressed throat and the desperate, furious scratching of Claudell's fingernails over the plastic casing of the robot's forearm.

"Hey," said the other boy, eyes adjusting to the gloom. His face had gone slack with fright, his skin jaundiced by the warm radiation emanating from the plastic blinds. "Hey, what the fuck!"

The other boy tugged on the robot's fist. It did not move, though the motors droned insistently against the added weight.

"It's fucking killing him!" the boy shouted again, this time with bright panic in his voice, tears springing to his eyes. "Tell it to let go! *Please!*"

Looking upward, James saw that Special Automatic was looking at him.

"Let go?" James asked.

Drawing back its arm, the machine launched Claudell's semiconscious body across the room, his back denting into moldy drywall. The boy collapsed in a spray of mold and paint flakes, gagging, white foam on his lips. Crying outright now, his friend set to dragging Claudell out of the dark room and away from its terrible occupant.

And James rose.

Lowering his forehead, the boy allowed his lip to worm out from between his teeth. In the trembling shadow of the box fan, his eyes had become dark stars. He clenched his fingers together into tight fists and heard the grinding of plastic as Special Automatic did the same.

Things felt different.

Not blinking, James stared silently as the boys fled the room. Above and behind him, the machine shivered with its own pent-up power. The front door slammed shut a second later and the apartment was silent again.

James walked to the bedroom doorway. Alone and safe, his hands had begun to tremble. He was experiencing an unfamiliar feeling, a shift in the topography of his world. The electrical flash of another R-word had left its imprint in his mind.

Respect—

Skinny Mike lunged in from the hallway, spider-fast, and delivered an open-handed slap that connected across James's temple, slamming the boy's head against the door frame. Reeling, spinning and blinking, James saw his older brother's gaunt silhouette canting over him as he fell to the floor.

"The fuck did you just *do*?" asked Mike.

James opened his eyes, leaning his head against the ratty, overstuffed La-Z-Boy in the living room. Mike crouched across from him, knees on his elbows, exposing the puckered veins of his inner forearms. Beside him, Delia lay languidly on the couch, a cigarette clasped lightly between her middle and index finger, one leg up on the coffee table, showing off her thin, bruised thigh and a glimpse of red panties.

"You little fuck," said Mike. "You little *fuck*."

Delia giggled, blowing smoke at the ceiling.

"Right?" asked Mike. "Why didn't he tell me he had that shit? You trying to hide this from me?"

The boy pushed stiff hair away from his face, fingers pausing on the tender bruise spreading across his forehead.

"No, Mikey," said James.

This was true. Until now, Mike had never shown genuine interest in his younger brother. James fundamentally did not understand how anything he did could be of concern to his older brother, or possibly to anyone.

"Okay, that thing is fucking amazing," said Mike, half to himself.

"What is it?" asked Delia, scratching her thigh with gold-colored fingers. "It's a robot, right?"

"Yes," said James.

"Can it walk?" asked Mike.

"I think so."

"Where'd you get it?"

"I made it."

"Jesus. What do you call it?"

James said nothing. After a long moment, Mike's face darkened, and, like a snake striking, he snatched up the TV remote and threw it at James. It hit the younger boy in the chest like a stone. James's hand flew to the spot of this new injury.

Quietly, he answered. "I call him Special," he said.

"Special? Special what? Special ed?"

"Special Automatic," said James.

Mike squawked a laugh. Reaching behind his back, he fingered out the black hunk of metal that lived there. Leaning forward again, he turned the snub-nosed pistol over in his fingers. James could smell sweat and cigarette smoke and gun oil.

"You named it like my gun? My .38?" Mike asked, a coathanger grin wedging into his flaccid, acne-scarred cheeks.

James nodded slowly.

"You gotta be fucking kidding me," said Mike.

Delia pushed a palm lightly against Mike's narrow shoulder.

"I think it's sweet," she sighed. "He wants to be like you."

Mike ignored the placating hand, leveling his eyes on James.

"That thing in there ain't a gun," said Mike. "Nobody

would be fucking stupid enough to give you a gun. That'd be like giving a gun to a monkey. Are you a bad mother-fucker, Jimmy? You a killer?"

James shook his head.

"Fucking killer monkey," murmured Delia, lips moving around the cigarette as she inhaled, her wheezing laugh pushing a haze of smoke toward the ceiling.

"No. You're not," continued Mike. "But I am."

James watched his older brother with wide unblinking eyes.

Although the younger boy had never been interesting to his older brother, the same was not true in reverse. Even if just for survival, James had paid a lot of attention to his older brother, especially to the job Mike did for the bald man, flexing his wasted muscles as he attempted to extract drug money from the corner dealers. And James had seen the power radiating from the small black weapon tucked into the back of his brother's jeans.

That was something James had paid quite a lot of attention to.

"How smart is it?" asked Mike.

James paused, lower lip twitching as he thought about the question. "Smarter than it looks, I guess," he murmured.

"Can it follow orders?" asked Mike.

James nodded.

Mike grinned wider, his scarred cheeks collapsing into a wrinkled moonscape.

"Then get your Special Automatic ready," he said. "And

make sure it can walk and move its arms and shit. Make sure it does what you say."

Mike stubbed out a cigarette in an overflowing ashtray and leaned back into the couch, draping an arm absent-mindedly across Delia's crotch, thinking.

"Why?" ventured James, watching his brother closely.

" 'Cause," said Mike, turning to Delia and blowing a last plume of smoke out the side of his mouth. He smiled at her, and saw that smile reciprocated with nervous anticipation. "We're gonna rob a bank with it."

The next day, just outside the First Niagara Bank, James tugged lightly on Special Automatic's arm. The machine paused, looking down at the boy. Although he had put on a ski mask, the boy's eyes were dry and dull with fear.

"Protect me," whispered James.

"Okay, James," said the machine, its smooth mouth area glowing yellow.

"Now go inside," added James.

Special Automatic turned and walked directly through the safety glass of the bank's front door.

Mouth muffled by a balaclava, Mike exclaimed his approval. James followed them both through curling leaves of fractured glass in the twisted door frame. He walked alone to the middle of the bank lobby as customers scattered, his head down, feeling diminutive and silly—a little kid along for the ride.

To hide the robot's true nature, James had pulled a matching balaclava over its head and duct-taped the remains of an old jacket and pants over its thin metal limbs. Wearing a ball cap cocked to one side, the machine looked like a gaunt, skeletal man, its movements unnaturally jerky yet surging with a terrible strength.

Mike's gun was already out, and the bank lobby deserted.

"The counter," James whispered, and Special Automatic staggered forward, crunching over cubes of glass, locking both hands under the teller's impenetrable window and lifting. The bulletproof glass shattered immediately, and the entire marble countertop buckled and rose away from its wooden mooring.

Somewhere, someone screamed.

Shoving the countertop to the side, Special Automatic dropped the glittering mess across the tile floor, leaving a cringing employee exposed, her forearms crossing over her face like the narrow slats of a boardwalk.

Fluorescent light glinted from Mike's drawn .38 special as he charged through the mess, an empty black duffel bag flapping in his free hand. Standing in the lobby, eyes on the floor, James could hear Mike laughing maniacally between shouted curses and threats, darting back and forth between tellers and registers, his sack growing as he filled it with bundles of cash.

Special Automatic waited patiently near the wreckage of the teller's desk, not moving. The boy and the robot exchanged a look, the room silent save for the panicked breaths of a teller hiding out of sight. In that moment, James realized he felt safe. It was if he were watching a movie. Reaching up, he put a hand over his chest and felt that his heart was not beating especially hard.

Thirty seconds later, Special Automatic tore a metal security door open and the three of them loped across the parking lot to where Mike had parked a stolen car. Even with his incredible strength, Special struggled to carry the now bloated duffel bag. The robot, still dressed ridiculously, was barely able to fit inside the car.

"That was fucking sick," said Mike, breathing hard, starting the engine with a crank of his wrist, eyes wet with excitement. "We should do it again tomorrow."

Ever since the robbery that afternoon, James had felt strange. The usual haze of fear had somehow evaporated. It did not touch him, not even when he entered the crumbling apartment he shared with his brother. Normally, James saw each room as a series of escape routes or low places where he could be out of the way—places where he could be small.

But now he felt nothing. He saw only paint peeling.

Special Automatic stood in the living room like a statue. He had been stripped of the goofy clothing, but the residue of duct tape remained on his casing, and he was still wearing the sideways ball cap. The machine watched impassively as Skinny Mike upended the duffel bag on the couch and laid down on a pungent layer of cash.

He wallowed there for a while, a look of sublime happiness on his sallow face.

Finally, lighting a cigarette, Mike sat up, his freckled shoulder blades knifing out of a stained wifebeater. The balaclava had been pushed up onto his sweaty forehead, and he was wearing a ludicrous grin. A drug kit lay on the coffee table—made of greasy black leather with a golden zipper like clenched teeth.

James was kneeling on the carpet across from his brother, one arm resting on the scabby La-Z-Boy recliner, letting the mild heat from Special Automatic's battery wash over him from above.

"Do you want a TV dinner?" he asked Mike quietly.

"No, Jimmy," said Mike, glancing at him with annoyance. "Fuck, man. Can't you knock off that pussy shit even for a second? We just robbed a *bank*!"

Mike burst into laughter, cigarette trapped between two fingers in his cupped hand, uneven coils of smoke rising in hiccups over his mouth.

"Holy shit, dude," he said, croaking as he inhaled smoke. "Holy shit. Wait'll I tell Connor. He's gonna freak the fuck out."

"Connor?" asked the boy.

"My boss, dipshit."

James knew the bald enforcer was a real criminal. The man had never respected Mike, would never respect him, most likely. He would use him, instead.

A frown creased Skinny Mike's face, the expression

zigzagging where his nose had been broken and never healed right. His small eyes were trained on James, sensing disagreement.

"Yeah," added Mike. "I'm gonna tell *everybody*. And nobody's gonna fuck with me ever again. You got a problem with that?"

Placing his palms flat on his thighs, James was quiet. He understood now that the money was not important to his brother. It was the implication of having the money that was important.

It was the respect, of course.

The silence spun away from him, a blank canvas on which Mike's diseased mind began to conjure unspoken insults.

"What are you thinking right now, dipshit?"

Feeling a tightness in the back of his throat, James stood up to leave, but Mike's thin fingers lashed out in that surprising, quick way he had. With a jerk, Mike dragged James forward and hooked an elbow behind his head. He pressed James's face hard against the coffee table.

Then harder.

"This whole neighborhood is gonna know that Skinny Mike has got a friend now. And he is one *bad motherfucker*."

With that, Mike pressed a bony forearm over the boy's cheek. In his cupped hand the cigarette still burned, inches from James's face. Squeezing his eyes closed against the smoke, James swallowed a cough. He silently wished for the strength to put a stop to this. But it was an impotent wish, long unfulfilled.

"Isn't that right, Special?" asked Mike, cackling. "Are you a bad motherfucker?"

In the acrid darkness, under the crushing pressure, Mike's words loomed huge. James felt as though he were a small figure crouched behind his own closed eyes, gazing up at the black movie screen of his life.

"Put together by a fucking genius *retard*—"

The words stopped as the air seemed to shiver. The pressure disappeared from the side of James's face. Eyes opening, he watched a last ribbon of smoke curl away. There had been a hard, wet sound—like stomping in a mud puddle with rain boots on.

James sat up and rubbed his eyes, blinking tears away.

Protect me, James had said before the robbery.

Okay, James, said the machine.

But James hadn't said from what, and he hadn't said when to stop.

James scrambled back from the coffee table, feeling a warm dollop of wetness sticking his shirt to his shoulder blade. With his back pressed against the La-Z-Boy, James pulled his knees up to his chest, saw the room, and focused on taking the kind of deep breaths that were supposed to help when a seizure was coming. With one hand, he reached up and stroked the lump of smooth plastic that bulged behind his ear.

He tried, but could not look away from his brother.

Skinny Mike was lying upside down across the back of the couch, flung there when Special Automatic had planted a fist into the side of his face. The metal knuckles had pushed a fishbowl dent into the side of Mike's head. Head cocked unnaturally, eyes and mouth open, Mike looked surprised—almost amused—as the ashtray-sized dent in his head pooled with blood. His jaw worked soundlessly.

Special Automatic's plastic knuckles glistened.

The humming of the machine was comforting to James, especially over the goldfish-kiss sounds his brother's lips were making as he gasped for air. Eyes rolling in their sockets, trying to blink, Mike's unfocused gaze settled on James.

"Yuh . . . *yoo*," he slurred.

James stared back. He put a hand over his heart and felt that the muscle was not beating especially hard.

Some intangible quality of Mike's eyes had changed, a softened focus, and James knew his brother would never be the same. The boy did not think he would be crouching on the fire escape again anytime soon. He wondered what his mother would say.

"Special?" asked James, turning, his voice breaking.

The boy looked up to where the towering machine stood, silly cap on its head, arms hanging like meat hooks. James carefully circled around the kneeling coffee table. He faced the machine without expression, both of them dark and still.

"Thank you," he said.

James stepped forward and wrapped his arms around the machine's legs. While he hugged it, the soft yellow LEDs under the machine's chin glowed. In a rumbling voice, it spoke: "You're welcome, James."

Thump. Thump. Thump.

The boy could not lift Skinny Mike on his own, despite the nickname, but he thought it best to leave Special Automatic out of view and do this part himself. So he was holding his brother's limp body by the armpits, pulling him down the stairs step by step.

At the bottom, James dragged his mute brother down the main hallway and through a side door to the alley. Making sure nobody was watching, he laid him beside a dumpster that squatted on an oil slick of its own offal.

This is where the ambulance people would find him.

"Nnngh," said Mike, eyes half-open.

They might wonder what happened to him. They might not. Even if the police bothered to come looking, they wouldn't care much about a dirtbag like Skinny Mike. Assumptions would be made. Attention would be paid elsewhere.

Drug deal gone wrong. Case closed.

The money from the robbery was safely hidden in a hole in the apartment ceiling. Only Special Automatic could reach it.

"Get well soon, Mikey," said James. "I'll be here when you're better."

Skinny Mike had no response. Instead, he took deep

breaths, mouth half-open, a sheen of drool collecting on his lower lip.

James left his brother in the alley and went back up the stairs. Reentering the apartment, he closed the door and leaned against it, taking a deep breath of his own.

It felt safer in here, as if a dangerous animal had been removed. Which was true.

James picked up his brother's prepaid phone and dialed 9-1-1. After a moment listening, he lifted the phone to Special Automatic.

"Hello," said the machine. "I need an ambulance on Brown and Millvale. There's a man hurt, by a dumpster."

James hung up the phone and disassembled it, dropping the pieces as he walked through the apartment.

Although what happened had been sudden, James felt confident. With the comfortable bulk of Special Automatic looming over him, he sat down in Mike's La-Z-Boy. Lower lip twitching, James thought about what he wanted to do next.

And for the first time, he had the power to do it.

The corner boys watched in disbelief as the handicapped kid shuffled up the street. With his twisted lip, downcast eyes, and that shuffling duck walk, they relished whatever insanity had convinced him to show up.

Eyeing his friends, Marin hopped up and ambled down the sidewalk.

Marin had heard the retard had built a robot that had choked Claudell nearly to death but promptly dismissed it as made-up bullshit. Put on the line, even Claudell's best friend had admitted that the fight hadn't gone the way he described, telling them later that Claudell had slipped and fell and they'd made up the story to cover for it.

"Hey, Jimmy," called Marin in a singsong voice, standing at the corner of the alleyway with his thumbs tucked into his pants. Marin had grown up with this weird kid and fought him countless times. But even if James was a mental case, it was also true he was from the same street. He deserved his one chance to run.

"You finally lost your fucking mind?"

James stopped at the other side of the alley's mouth, keeping his eyes aimed at his feet. He had considered looking up but decided it wouldn't matter. Struggling to push authority into his voice, James spoke.

"I'm here to collect. For Connor."

Marin's mouth split into a wide, gold-flecked grin. One hand flew to his forehead in disbelief and the other, out of habit, to the 9mm Glock tucked into his waistband.

"You are fucking crazy," he said. Leaving the weapon tucked, he pointed at James. "For real. Who's making you do this?"

James pulled his gaze up from the sidewalk and planted his dark eyes on Marin's disbelieving, half-smiling face.

"Give me the money," said James, inhaling. "And nobody will get hurt."

Smile gone, Marin drew his gun. Behind him, four more boys spread out like jackals, eager to see the outcome of this joke gone wrong. Stone-faced, Marin aimed his weapon and took a step closer.

"You wanna die?" he asked James, unaware of the silver arm snaking out of the alleyway. Special Automatic clamped a fist onto Marin's chest, audibly snapping his collarbone, and yanked his flailing body into the alley. Two expensive sneakers remained on the sidewalk, unlaced, perfectly clean, and still facing James.

Marin's weapon fired once, wildly, into the air.

James turned and quietly walked back to the row house where he lived. He did not run because he knew it would cause the corner boys to chase him. Instead, he let them rush into the alley to find Marin.

As he walked, the look on James's face was thoughtful.

In the alleyway, Marin was pressed against the brick wall, face-to-face with an expressionless monster made of scuffed plastic and metal. With a shake, it knocked the boy's head against the brick and then everything began to feel like a dream.

"Leave the money in Mike's mail slot," it said, voice purring, reasonable and calm. "From now on. Do you understand?"

Marin opened his mouth and accidentally coughed blood onto the thing's face. He could tell something was fucked in his chest. His neck felt like someone was fishing a red-hot wire coat hanger through it and trying to unlock something in his rib cage.

"Yuh—yes," gasped Marin, heels scraping against the wall through his socks. "Yes, *fuck*."

The hulking contraption dropped Marin to the ground in front of his astonished friends. Motors whining with power, it surveyed the boys without fear. Then, it shuffled away with slow steps, saying nothing, its unnaturally long arms hanging at its sides.

Marin waved at his boys.

"No," he croaked. "Leave it."

A block away, James walked into the row house and headed for the metal back door. He noticed the cloying smell of perfume and cigarette smoke in the long hallway, but dismissed it. Reaching the door, he met Special Automatic in the alley. As he turned to lead the machine back inside, James felt fingers digging into his shoulder. Someone had been waiting for him, hiding on the stairs.

Someone strong.

"Where's your brother?" asked Connor.

The bald man's bulk consumed most of the hallway, and he was flanked by two of his leather-jacketed bodyguards. Behind them, James heard the scrape of high heels on the lacquered wooden floor and saw Delia's thin legs where she was waiting on the stairwell. She must have led these men here.

James said nothing, so Connor jabbed him in the shoulder with two fingers.

"Answer me, kid," he said.

And in that moment, the boy raised his eyes.

"Mike had an accident," he said. "He's at West Penn."

James's hands had closed into fists.

"I'll take his route," he continued, looking up at the bald man. "I can do it."

Connor's eyes went wide.

"What?" he asked.

"I told you," hissed Delia, from the stairs. "The kid is crazy. Dangerous."

Connor pointed at the looming piece of machinery in the doorway, frozen in place but humming with potential.

"You retarded? They'll eat you alive on the street. No science fair project is going to ever change that."

There it was again. That word. Across all the years, and in all its variations, it had never lost its pinch.

Special Automatic turned to look down at Connor. The big man took an involuntary step back, sinking deeper into the cool, gloomy hallway. The two brutes behind him pulled weapons from their jackets and aimed them at the machine.

"No," said Connor. "Aim at the kid."

Two guns nosed toward James.

"How smart is that thing?" Connor asked.

"Mike said it does whatever he tells it," called Delia from the stairs, voice echoing through a forest of leather jackets. "Calls it Special Automatic."

Slowly, the great plastic head turned to James.

"He's my friend," said the boy, quietly. "He protects me."

"Your *friend*?" asked the bald man. "The kind of friend who was gonna help your dumbshit brother rob a bank?"

So Connor didn't know that the robbery had already taken place. Mistaking James's relief for surprise, the bald man smiled, his uneven teeth stained with nicotine.

"Take Frankenstein," Connor said, stepping back between his men. "If the kid tries to talk to it, shoot him."

"Please," said James, putting a hand on the big machine's scarred plastic forearm. "Don't take him—"

The side of a gun popped James against the temple, jarring the lump of plastic tucked behind his ear and spreading black ink over his vision. He watched as the hallway rolled to the side, the floor coming up to meet him. After his face met the wooden floor, he wasn't aware of much. Just a glow of yellow from somewhere high above. Gentle words. A husky synthetic voice.

"It will be okay, James," said Special Automatic, knees dipping as the men wrestled the machine to the floor. "You are strong—"

The big fucking robot had not worked for shit since they took it from the kid. Connor's guys had to drag it out of the hallway and cram its limp body into the back of an SUV. As impressive as it was when it stood around, the thing seemed pathetic without juice—a rag doll made of metal and plastic, mute, its scarred-up face lolling around on its loose neck like a fucking cripple.

Things were better once they had it back in the bar. Not

that it was working, but at least Connor could have a drink while they tried to figure it out.

Making some calls, he'd scraped up the closest thing he could find to a professional. The skinny guy with glasses who had showed up—an addict, probably—was hunched over the machine where it lay across the pool table. His Adam's apple bobbed as he tapped at the machine with electrician's tools.

"The fuck is wrong with it?" called Connor.

The tweaker engineer just shook his head.

From the corner of the bar, one of the guys called out from a game of poker. "Give it some juice for chrissake, ya fuckin' egghead."

Eyeglasses glinting, the engineer glanced up. "It's got power, all right," he said. "Everything is online. I'm trying to figure out why it's not *doing* anything."

Connor ran fingers through his thick black hair, considering the shot of whiskey in his other hand. Something didn't feel right. The machine was giving off a low humming sound that felt like atomic radiation.

This was turning into a bad scene.

For no reason, Connor's mind turned to how the boy's hands had collapsed into fists in that dark hallway. That was weird for a kid who never took his eyes off the ground, who never smiled or looked you in the face.

Kid should have been more afraid.

"It's like it's catatonic," murmured the engineer. "Brain-dead."

Delia pocketed her cell phone and hopped off the pool

table, her sagging breasts bouncing around in a top that was too tight and too bright.

"All right," she said. "I'm out of here. I gotta go see Mike. And I can't stand looking at that . . . thing, no more today."

Connor nodded, turned back to his whiskey. Tipping it to the side, he watched the amber liquid streak the thick glass.

"Can't you turn off that fucking *hum*?!" Connor shouted to nobody in particular. He threw back the shot, letting the heat of it course down his throat.

The bar door squeaked on its hinges as Delia pushed it open. For an instant, the empty whiskey glass took on the blue gleam of daylight. And then the girl was screaming her fucking head off.

It was the kid.

James stood in the doorway, his small frame silhouetted by bright sunlight. Inside the dim bar, the guys were already up and aiming their guns. The tweaker stayed hunched over Special Automatic, curious and a little annoyed, pushing up his glasses and squinting into the rectangle of light.

"Jesus Christ," spat Delia, pushing past the kid into daylight. "You scared the shit outta me, Jimmy. I hope you get what you deserve."

Her heels clip-clopped away into the parking lot, door closing behind her.

"Special Automatic," said the kid's shadow.

Sighing, Connor leaned against the bar. It wasn't fun

anymore. In Connor's opinion, some people were too fucking stupid or stubborn to know when they'd lost. Some
people had to be hurt in order to learn. No big deal. But
with a thick-skulled kid like this, Connor couldn't take any
pleasure in it.

"Bring him inside," he said, tired, motioning to his
bodyguards and setting the shot glass down on the bar. It
made a startlingly loud *thock*. Connor looked at his hand,
surprised at how loud it was. Then, in his peripheral vision,
he saw that it wasn't his glass that had made the sound. It
was the tweaker engineer's skull shattering as he bounced
off the concrete ceiling over the pool table.

The shadow in the doorway had one hand raised.

On the pool table, the monstrous machine called Special
Automatic also had one hand raised. Connor gaped at the
body of the engineer as it landed in a limp heap.

The boy walked farther inside, into the light.

His warped lower lip was pulled to the side, flashing
his lower teeth. As he thrust his arms out to his sides, the
machine on the pool table rose up in all its horrible glory.

"No," said Connor.

Suddenly animate, the machine lunged off the pool table
toward Connor's men, stepping through their flashing gunshots. In a swooping motion, Special Automatic flung the
two former bouncers into a mirrored wall that exploded
into a silver waterfall of razored glass.

Across the room, the boy's hands pushed at empty air.

"No," mouthed the bald man.

Illuminated by the shivering light of the swinging pool table lamp, James was looking at Connor now. Looking him right in the goddamn eyes. And behind the boy, a shadow rose, nearly seven feet tall, thrumming with raw power.

"You?" asked Connor. "You control that thing? Like a puppet?"

That's why it didn't work. It had nobody controlling it.

Connor noticed the lump behind the boy's ear—the battery pack for some kind of an implant. It was why they called the kid handicapped. He had this piece of hardware stuck in his head to make his brain work. And maybe more than that.

The boy walked forward and the machine matched his steps.

"You nearly killed your own brother," said Connor.

He knew the words were true as soon as they left his lips.

Special Automatic casually picked up one end of the pool table and flung it out of the way, the corner of it smashing through the far wall. Connor felt the bar pressing hard against the small of his back. No more room to run. He put his hands up, noticed with wonder that they were shaking.

"Hey, don't," he begged, surprising himself. "You don't have to."

Now the kid was standing only a couple feet away, his shoulders still slumped. The machine was a dark tower of hell behind him. Connor felt the strength go out of his legs. Knees buckling, he lowered himself down into an awkward kneel. He put his palms flat on the glittering tile and pulled his head back so he could look up at the kid.

The boy stood there, expectantly.

"What is it? What can I do?" asked Connor.

"James is your new partner," said the machine, voice low. "James is a bad motherfucker."

"Y-yeah," stuttered Connor. "Okay."

"Say it," said the machine.

"J-James . . . ," said Connor, swallowing, licking his lips. Nearby, one of his guys was bloody and weeping. The other one wasn't moving at all.

"Look at me," said James, softly.

It was the first time Connor had heard the kid speak with authority. The low commanding tone snapped him back into focus. This wasn't a conversation, he realized. This was about survival now.

Kneeling in the remains of his bar, the bald man put his shaking hands up and locked his eyes on the boy. A brand-new future was coming to life in his mind, unimaginable a moment ago. When he spoke, his voice was hollow with fear and respect.

"Kid," he said, "you are a *bad motherfucker*."

And James smiled.

ACKNOWLEDGMENTS

Growing up, I dreamed of writing the sort of fantastic short stories I so often read in *The Magazine of Fantasy and Science Fiction, Analog,* and *Amazing Stories.* I thank my high school English teacher, Mr. Paul Dykes, for facilitating that dream by reading and editing my early attempts with barely a wry smile. (And my thanks also to Three B's used bookstore in Tulsa, Oklahoma, for the endless supply of reading material.) Appreciation goes to my literary agent, Laurie Fox, for always advocating. And heartfelt thanks to my editors at Vintage, who helped beat this collection into shape, including Andrea Robinson, Andrew Weber, and Edward Kastenmeier. So many facets of my life, friends, and family have gone into these stories, and I must thank all of those people for putting up with me—especially Anna, Coraline, and Conrad.

ROBOPOCALYPSE

Not far into our future, the dazzling technology that runs our world turns against us. Controlled by a childlike— yet massively powerful—artificial intelligence known as Archos, the global network of machines on which our world has grown dependent suddenly becomes an implacable, deadly foe. At Zero Hour—the moment the robots attack—the human race is almost annihilated, but as its scattered remnants regroup, humanity for the first time unites in a determined effort to fight back. This is the oral history of that conflict, told by an international cast of survivors who experienced this long and bloody confrontation with the machines. Brilliantly conceived and amazingly detailed, *Robopocalypse* is an action-packed epic with chilling implications about the real technology that surrounds us.

Science Fiction

ROBOGENESIS

It's been three years since the global uprising of the world's robots, three long years in which ordinary people waged a guerrilla war that saved humankind from the brink of annihilation. But a horrific new enemy has emerged, and the resistance is called to fight once again. In a world where humanity and technology are pushed to the breaking point, their one hope may reside with their former enemy—Archos R-14.

Science Fiction

AMPED

Daniel H. Wilson masterfully envisions a stunning world where superhuman technology and humanity clash in surprising—and thrilling—ways. It's the near future, and scientists have developed implants that treat brain dysfunction—and also make recipients capable of super-human feats. Exploiting societal fears of the newly enhanced, politicians pass a set of laws to restrict the rights of "amplified" humans, instantly creating a new persecuted underclass known as "amps." On the day that the Supreme Court upholds the first of these laws, twenty-nine-year-old schoolteacher Owen Gray is forced into hiding, only dimly aware of the latent powers he pos-sesses. To escape imprisonment and to find out who he really is, Owen seeks out a community in Oklahoma where, it is rumored, a group of the most enhanced amps may be about to change the world—or destroy it.

Science Fiction

VINTAGE BOOKS
Available wherever books are sold.
www.vintagebooks.com

AMATKA
by Karin Tidbeck

Vanja, an information assistant, is sent from her home city of Essre to the austere, wintry colony of Amatka with an assignment to collect intelligence for the government. Immediately she feels that something strange is going on: people act oddly in Amatka, and citizens are monitored for signs of subversion. Intending to stay just a short while, Vanja falls in love with her housemate, Nina, and prolongs her visit. But when she stumbles on evidence of a growing threat to the colony and a cover-up by its administration, she embarks on an investigation that puts her at tremendous risk. In Karin Tidbeck's world, everyone is suspect, no one is safe, and nothing—not even language, nor the very fabric of reality—can be taken for granted. *Amatka* is a beguiling and wholly original novel about freedom, love, and artistic creation by a captivating voice.

Fiction

THE GONE-AWAY WORLD
by Nick Harkaway

Gonzo Lubitsch and his best friend have been inseparable since birth. They grew up together, they studied kung fu together, they rebelled in college together, and they fought in the Go Away War together. Now, with the world in shambles and dark, nightmarish clouds billowing over the wastelands, they have been tapped for an incredibly perilous mission. But they quickly realize that this assignment is more complex than it seems, and before it is over they will have encountered everything from mimes, ninjas, and pirates to one ultrasinister mastermind whose only goal is world domination.

Fiction

THE VORRH
by B. Catling

Next to the colonial town of Essenwald sits the Vorrh, a
vast—perhaps endless—forest. It is a place of demons and
angels, of warriors and priests. Sentient and magical, the
Vorrh bends time and wipes memory. Legend has it that
the Garden of Eden still exists at its heart. Now a rene-
gade English soldier aims to be the first human to traverse
its expanse. Armed with only a strange bow, he begins his
journey, but some fear the consequences of his mission, and
a native marksman has been chosen to stop him. Around
them swirl a remarkable cast of characters, including a
cyclops raised by robots and a young girl with tragic curi-
osity, as well as historical figures such as writer Raymond
Roussel and photographer Edward Muybridge. While fact
and fiction blend, the hunter will become the hunted, and
everyone's fate hangs in the balance, under the will of the
Vorrh.

Fiction

ALSO AVAILABLE
The Erstwhile by B. Catling

VINTAGE BOOKS
Available wherever books are sold.
www.vintagebooks.com